NAIJA LOVE STORIES

NAIJA LOVE STORIES

BY

OLA AWONUBI

Naija Love Stories

Copyright © 2018: Ola Awonubi

First Printed in United Kingdom 2018

Published by Conscious Dreams Publishing
www.consciousdreamspublishing.com

Edited by Rhoda Molife
www.molahmedia.com

ISBN: 978-1-912551-36-1

DEDICATIONS

∞

To Debbie and Robert, 2 young Nigerian students who braved cold weather and cold hearts, pressing through to make England home for their children. Thanks Dad - wish you were here to see this. Thanks Mum – for your love, strength and continued prayers.

∞

To Stella Lillian Trott, the inspiration behind my first literary scribblings - thanks for the Enid Blyton books and your apple pie. You are always in my heart.

ACKNOWLEDGEMENTS

൧

Thank you to the Conscious Dreams Publishing Team: Daniella Blechner - Book Journey Mentor, Rhoda Molife - Editor and Oksana Kosovan – Typesetter.

To Big Field Digital – thank you for designing my book cover.

Jacob Ross, Joy Francis, Yejide Kilanko, Irenosen Okojie, Valerie Brandes, Emma Shercliff, Bibi Bakare-Yusuf, Sifa Asani Gowon, Belema Olagbemi, Sade Adeniran, Abidemi Sanusi, Dawn Promislow and Afam Akeh – thank you for your support and encouragement during my writing journey.

To Yinka, Kem, Sope, Femi and Lou - thanks for believing in me.

To my wider family both in Brighton and Lagos – thank you for *everything*.

To my Pastors and church family at KICC, my coach and dream team – thank you for your inspiration and for keeping the faith with me.

To all of you that have helped to turn my dream into a reality – I thank you from the bottom of my heart.

TABLE OF CONTENTS

ॐ

ONE

THE PINK HOUSE

℘

M y mother always used to say that we lived on the decent part of the street where the houses had bigger yards and cars but smaller families. The bottom end was for those whose social standing meant that they had no choice but to pack themselves, and sometimes their extended families, into rented rooms in small, squalid bungalows.

Opposite us was one of these unfortunate habitations painted the exact colour of my favourite bubblegum. Warm rosy pink. Its window shutters and doors reminded me of an old woman's mouth - an odd selection of different colours, faded, crooked, some missing. My father was an architect and believed that the town planning people should have long pulled it down and built a decent house. He said it was an eyesore, a boil on the face of humanity and an absolute monstrosity. My father loved to confuse us with big words.

My mother was a governor at my school, a teacher at another and lay preacher at the local Anglican church. Her stance on the matter of the house went a step further than that of my father's. She believed that the house's presence on the street was like the serpent in paradise, a cancerous legacy that lay dormant and if not dealt with, was certain to threaten all the decent families in the neighbourhood and ultimately the whole of society.

'I don't know why we stand for it. We complain, and the police promise to deal with it – yet nothing is done.' This was my mother's mantra.

I was eight years old then and wondered why she felt so strongly about the house across the road. However, I had long learnt that when children asked questions that adults did not want to answer, they were sent off to their studies.

Our sitting room had large French windows that opened onto the verandah letting in the noises, music and laughter that floated in from the street. I used to spend hours looking out of the window at the pink house wishing I could go inside to see the secrets it held - the secrets no adult ever spoke about. The number of women that lived there varied widely. I had counted often, but always gave up in the end. Even though I didn't know their names, I knew their faces and I had given them all nicknames. There was the dark, plump one I called Fatty, and the tall, slim one I called The Mermaid because she always wore her hair in long plaits. I called one The Jackson Girl because of her big afro, like the Jackson Five wore on the cover of their album. There were always visitors coming and going and lots of cars and loud music. Especially in the evening. I asked my mother why they only had male visitors and she told me to mind my own business.

I wanted to look like the girls in the house. Their hair would either be pressed straight until it shone or plaited in the most intricate styles. They wore the latest clothes and their makeup was really cool. Some afternoons they would bring a radio out onto the front veranda and dance to the music. The first time I heard Fela and his afro-beat music was on that veranda. I was ten and I still remember the words to 'Lady' very clearly:

> *'If you call an African woman*
> *African woman no go 'gree*
> *She go say*
> *She go say*
> *I be lady o*
> *She go say*
> *I be lady o'*

Then they would sway and jiggle and lose themselves in the drumbeat. At the peak of the heat, the girls would enjoy the cool shade of the big tree that hung over their veranda, sleeping, plaiting hair or just talking. I did catch a couple of them crying one day and I was surprised because they were all so beautiful and had so many friends.

One evening, mother ran out of salt so she asked me to go down the road to get some from Mama George who sold everything from buttons to kerosene. I saw The Mermaid getting out of a big, dark-green car driven by an army man. Another older army man, his uniform covered with badges of some sort, sat at the back. She stood in front of the house and watched the car until it disappeared as tears filled her eyes. I asked her what was wrong.

'I'm sure your mother wouldn't want you talking to me,' replied The Mermaid.

The large, gold hoops in her ears fascinated me, and so did her tears.

'My mother is at home,' I responded matter of factly.

She shook her head. 'You wouldn't understand. You are young.'

'I will be a teenager soon,' I retorted.

The Mermaid's voice lowered as if she was talking to herself. 'He wanted to marry me last week. I would have had a whole house, a car, my own driver and a houseboy to myself. I would have been a big Madam. Now he says he can no longer marry me because his Mrs will not allow him to take another wife. I don't even know if the bastard will come to see me anymore.'

I wanted to ask her what a bastard was but decided not to. 'How can he marry you if he already has a wife?'

She glared at me as if she was seeing me for the first time and hissed. 'Just go away you silly girl!'

I suddenly remembered that my mother had spat on the red sand in front of our veranda before I left and told me to be back before it dried – so I sprinted off to the shop.

⁊୦

The next and last person I saw cry in that house was The Jackson Girl. My parents had gone to a party and my aunt was looking after my baby brother upstairs, so I had the freedom to sit on our verandah and enjoy the cool early evening air. Several cars were parked outside the pink house and people were coming and going as usual. James Brown blared from the loudspeakers and the women were buying peppered chicken, soft drinks and beer from the street traders who set up their wares every night. I saw a car draw up and three people get out and walk towards the house – a man and a woman of about my parents' age dressed in traditional clothes, and a younger man in a modern shirt with trousers. They had to be visitors because I had never seen them before.

The young man knocked on the big, red door. One of the women came to open the door and the visitors pushed past her and went in. Then I heard shouting and screaming. Some of the men in the place rushed out, got into their cars and drove off. One was putting on his trousers. I saw The Jackson Girl run out of the house into the street screaming, pursued by the younger man who was carrying a big stick, who was in turn pursued by the man and woman who were my parents' age.

Now outside, the woman was shouting. 'Prostitutes! You lot have corrupted my child. She was a good girl before she came to Lagos! If the police don't come and shut this den of iniquity down I will burn it to the ground myself! This place is worse than Sodom and Gomorrah!'

There was a crowd of petty traders, self-righteous housewives and jobless youths forming in front of the house. The more educated peered through their curtains and shook their heads. I could sense this was going to be better than TV. The older man was holding the younger man, preventing him from going at The Jackson Girl with his stick. She now stood at a safe distance, hands folded across her chest.

'Leave me alone old man!' the young man cried. 'I paid bride price on her head and a week after the engagement she runs to Lagos to sell herself! What about the money I paid for her to learn dressmaking? What about the money I gave your family for her dowry eh?'

'I am sorry. Please, see my white hairs on my head and pity me. I'm not too proud to kneel before you. You are like my son. Forgive her and take her back.' The old man sounded forlorn.

'Forgive?! How can you expect me to take back a woman that has probably slept with half of Lagos? Everyone back home is laughing at me already. Do you think my family can survive any further shame?'

The crowd cheered and supported him.

'Yes Sah! Get your money back from the wicked girl!' someone yelled.

'Such a disgrace to her family!' a woman cried.

'She deserves to be stripped naked and made to walk down the street,' suggested one man earnestly.

'Burn the evil place down!' a housewife shouted, rallying the crowd.

The Jackson Girl had stopped crying and was now laughing. 'Hypocrites! If you were looking after your men do you think they would be coming to us?'

The crowd quietened and seeing that she had caught their attention, she became bolder. 'As for him...,' she pointed to the young man, 'I came to Lagos after I found out he was sleeping with my best friend. I said to myself he likes her because she has pressed her hair, speaks better English and wears nice clothes. I deserve better than a liar who would betray me with such a woman. At least now I get paid for betrayal.' She jeered and hissed at him.

Just as I thought the young man was going to chase after her again, I felt a sharp slap on my shoulder. I turned my head around to see my aunt standing behind me with her arms crossed.

'Get inside. NOW! If your mother...,'

She pulled me inside and sent me off to bed. I was annoyed at missing the rest of soap opera. When she came up a long time later to check on us, I had just one question.

'What does prostitute mean?'

'Go to sleep' was apparently the answer.

I tried again. 'So, what happened outside?' I could not see my aunt's face because the light was dim.

Her voice was laced with a hint of finality. 'The police came but they were too late. Now go to bed.'

ℰᴐ

The next morning, I woke up and saw that the pink house had been boarded up and the girls were sitting outside with their suitcases and bags. Some were crying.

'Why are they going?'

My mother's eyes were red. Her voice was heavy. 'It's a sad story. Apparently one of the girls died last night. Her fiancé came to get her and when she refused to go back with him…he had a knife and he…,' mother stopped and then shook her head. 'You ask too many questions! Get up and go and take a bath!'

I bathed in a daze, trying to understand what I had heard and seen the night before. Afterwards, for the first time in my young life, I refused breakfast. Within a few days, neighbours were saying that at night, they'd seen a girl with a huge afro sitting on the portico plaiting her hair and singing a Fela song. That scared me so I made sure that I never ran errands that would take me past the empty pink house after sundown. A few months later, they pulled the place down and replaced it with a house like ours. My father was happy that the town planners had finally seen sense and done the right thing. All that was needed now was for the other horrible houses on that side of the street to be taken down. Then, the street would attract good people.

ℰℴ

A few years later, in my teens, my mother became extra strict and said if she even saw me talking to a boy, she would kill me.

'That's what probably got that girl along that terrible path. Her mother wasn't strict enough. Well, I won't make that mistake,' she would tell me as she brandished a cane.

Through those tough teenage years, I often thought of the girls in the pink house with fondness. Sometimes I thought about where the other girls might have gone, especially The Mermaid. I wondered whether she had got her army man, a whole house, a car, her own driver and a houseboy all to herself.

TWO

THE GO-SLOW JOURNEY

ℰↄ

A bird flying over any of the three Lagos bridges would see long queues of cars that stretch out like a multi-coloured scarf across the blue sea. Like caged animals waiting to pounce, they sound their engines and honk their horns as tempers soar in the heavy heat.

All other cities around the world have traffic jams. Lagos has 'go-slow'. In the 70s, the Lagos State Government introduced a system called 'Odd and Even', where motorists with even-numbered registration plates could not drive on the days marked for odd-numbered cars and vice-versa. Most Lagosians just bought another car, rendering this solution like so many that were to follow, completely pointless.

On this day, Bayo Badejo, 25, bachelor with aspirations of a better existence than the one in which he found himself, left his extremely modest one room in the bungalow that he shared with twelve other families, and walked to the bus stop. He dreamt that one day he would have lots of money and a beautiful wife because obviously once money came, the women would follow. So, the most pressing issue on his mind was finding a job because he could not think of any more creative ways of avoiding the landlord and his other creditors. He sent up a prayer that this would be his last interview.

Bayo joined the crowd at the bus stop and felt his fragile optimism wilt at the sight of their frustrated resignation. He wondered how long he would have to wait in the boiling sun for a *Molue* or *Danfo*. Although these were the capital's answer to public transport, they were nothing but yellow pieces of metal with broken windows that sucked in air as they rattled down the road. Bayo was certain that in sophisticated countries like England and America, not even animals would be transported in such contraptions. However, like millions of others in this city, he did not have a choice but to use said contraptions to get around.

They did have the advantage of being the cheapest form of transportation going if you didn't want to take an *okada* - a motorbike - ironically named after one of the nation's airlines. He wondered what was more dangerous in Nigeria - flying in the air or flying down a road without a crash helmet, weaving around queues of cars, taunting death. Fatalities were inevitable especially after the Lagos Council Government had instituted a new rule that if a passenger got injured whilst being transported, the driver would be liable. Since hospital bills were notoriously steep, some *okada* drivers had developed the habit of abandoning injured and dying passengers alongside the motorbike and running away from the scene of the crime.

He recalled one such gruesome ending of a young woman's life. She must have been in her mid-twenties and she lay spread out on the road in the hot sun, her eyes opened to the heavens, her mouth full of blood. They found the baby she had tied on her back several meters away. It had made the go-slow worse as vehicles had to manoeuvre around the bodies until the mortuary van came. People shook their heads and said a prayer for them but minutes later they shrugged their shoulders and talked about the government, the rising cost of living, the lack of basic amenities or the latest highlife tune.

The long buses and vans were for the middle-class workers from banks and foreign companies and their children. You knew you had really made it if you had your own car, not a jalopy or an old banger, but a shiny Mercedes with a driver to ferry you and Madam around town. One day he would get his own car. It would be long and sleek and turn heads in the way a beautiful woman does. In fact, there was one standing tall and slim in the crowd. She was a shade of polished mahogany, a real African queen. Her light pink skirt suit hugged over the kind of curves and contours that young men like him could only stare at and dream about. Maybe she sensed his thoughts, because she turned and looked at him, her expression obscured by her large sunglasses, before turning back to the traffic.

Don't go there my friend. This one pass your level.

A lorry with the words 'E go better' written across the body, drove past blazing. Yes, things will get better one day.

That was what made people live in this crazy city. The dream that one day you could shift levels from *Molue* to 'middle-class' and then onto 'Big Man' status so you could sit in an air-conditioned car and look down at the people rushing to get into the yellow pieces of metal with broken windows that sucked in air as they rattled down the road.

The *Molue* showed up, clattering to a stop several meters away from the bus stop. Drivers were reluctant to park right at the bus stop because *Maja-Maja*, the vehicle police, lay in wait like foxes, ready to get bribes. The conductor, or *Agbero*, as nicknamed by Lagosians, stuck his head out of the battered passenger's door screeching out destinations.

'Lawanson! Ojuelegba! Idumota! Keffi!'

The crowd surged towards the vehicle, jumping over the street beggars and traders to squeeze inside. A woman put her son through one of the windows and Bayo found himself jostled and pushed until he managed a get a seat near a window. He was sandwiched between a plump lady carrying a bag of *ankara* - African print material – to his left and an old man to his right. Much to his delight, opposite him sat Miss Pink Suit and Sunglasses. Bayo had a chance to get a better look at the girl when she finally took the sunglasses off.

There was this joke about girls. God had created women on different days of the week. The ones He had created on Sunday, Monday and Tuesday were the loveliest. By the time it got to Saturday, He had run out of creative inspiration and the girls were not so pretty. This one was definitely created on Sunday. She was very beautiful with big, piercing eyes and plump, ripe lips that shimmered with dark, red lipstick. Her long braids gently rested on her shoulders as she pulled out a copy of Jackie Collins' *Lucky*. He felt he had to say something, as one educated person to another.

'Nice book.'

She looked up and starting from the top of his head, took in his grey, rumpled suit, his slightly worn shoes and briefcase, before twisting her lips and returning to her book. Bayo swallowed his shame and decided to open his briefcase and familiarise himself with the company he was hoping to work for. Well there was no harm in trying.

'Move out!' The Agbero gave the command and the *Molue*, having reached its full quota of passengers, teetered forward like a drunk and weaved down the road as passengers held onto their seats. The conductor started to collect his fares and stood in front of Bayo who gave him ten naira.

'*Oga*. Boss. I no get change o! Where are you getting down?'

Bayo glared at him. 'Idumota. Am I the Central Bank of Nigeria that I should find you change?'

The conductor collected a paper note from Miss Pink Suit and Sunglasses and shook his head.

'Doesn't anyone have the correct money this morning?'

Miss Pink Suit and Sunglasses shrugged. 'You are the conductor. Do your job and find change.'

The conductor looked at her and licked his lips. 'Sister. I really like you. Maybe one day when I have made some money, you could give someone like me a chance.'

Her eyes flashed contempt. 'Is your head in complete working order? Do I look as if I am the same level with you?'

The conductor leered at her again and rubbed his chest. 'One day I am going to buy my own bus like this one, and I will be rich, and you will see me and say, what a pity I missed my chance with that young man.'

'Just give me my change and go away! Horrible little man.'

The *Agbero* laughed. 'Where are you getting down?'

'Idumota,' she replied.

He turned to Bayo and handed him a ten naira note. 'I hereby pronounce you and this girl, husband and wife. I have joined you together and when you get to Idumota you can go buy some sweets and give her the change. Maybe you might even get a date.' He winked and moved to the next passenger leaving Bayo to stare helplessly at Miss Pink Suit and Sunglasses whose head was now back in her book.

The *Agbero* turned to the large woman next to him. 'Madam. You go pay double money o!'

'*You dey craze?* Are you totally mad?'

The *Agbero* shrugged. 'I could have fit two whole people in your seat Madam.'

'I do not have the money for two people! Was your mother's head OK when she had you?'

The *Agbero's* eyes turned bloodshot red. 'Don't abuse my mother! You can abuse me, but don't you dare abuse my mother! Am I the one that asked you to eat all the food in Lagos?'

Bayo saw Miss Pink Suit and Sunglasses trying not to laugh as the exchange escalated.

'Watch yourself o! I am old enough to be your mother!' shot back the plump lady.

'I don't have all day. Just pay me my money.'

'I have paid you your money and will not be paying a *kobo* more! Stupid boy! Look at his face like a hungry bush rat!'

Even the grumpy passengers laughed. The *Agbero* shook his head and moved on, promising to be back to deal with the lady. The next customers informed him that they were 'staff', meaning they were friends of the driver or fellow *Agberos* and therefore were absolved of paying the fare. The *Agbero* shouted to the driver. 'We have staff here and I can see some army men at the back as well.'

The driver started shouting and cursing his luck. 'Why is the bus attracting all the freeloaders in Lagos?'

One of the policemen spoke up. 'My friend. Who are you calling freeloaders? We are entitled to free transport.'

The driver hissed. 'There are many things that the police think they are entitled to.'

A woman laughed, saw one of the policemen glaring at her and hastily looked out of the window.

'I am in charge here,' declared the policeman as he sauntered up and down the bus, pushing past people too scared to complain. 'I can stop this bus now and start checking everyone's particulars.'

Everyone started talking at once.

'Please *Oga* policeman I am going to work. Don't mind the driver.'

'Yes o. I am an innocent market trader. I don't want police trouble.'

Bayo put his hands on his head as the policemen threatened to invoke every ounce of the powers of state on all the vulnerable masses in the bus. The last thing anyone wanted was police trouble especially when they had been sitting in a stationary bus for the past thirty minutes since they hit the go-slow on Carter Bridge. He wiped his brow, pulled at his tie and looked down at his suit, now rumpled and damp. His nose was now accustomed to the smell of peppers, fish and stale perspiration dripping down the bodies of his fellow passengers. Outside was a mini-market of people darting around the cars selling magazines, iced drinks, bread, pastries, CDs and clothes. The go-slow provided a captive set of customers.

Bayo heard a baby crying, probably irritated by the heat. Those who hadn't found a seat were sandwiched against each other in the aisle. The *Agbero* was shouting again asking someone to 'dress' forward.

A woman shouted. 'I can't move forward. We are not sardines you know!'

The *Agbero* was unrepentant. 'Madam. If you don't like it, you can always go and buy your car. Or ask your husband to buy one for you.'

'Shut up your stinking mouth,' hissed the woman. 'Driver! Warn this conductor of yours o!'

Bayo closed his eyes and tried to think.

Diamond Marketing Consultancy. Founded in 1975. Owned by Chief Cecil Ezimba. Branches in Lagos, Aba and Kano. Worked on major campaigns like Fight against Cholera, Eradication of Illiteracy, Gold Beer, Royal Cigarettes and Baby Care Nappies.

Speaking of nappies, the crying baby two seats behind him needed changing. He wrinkled his nose. That, the smells of the boiled egg the market woman opposite him was stuffing into her mouth and the cheap perfume of the bleached-face woman in the seat behind, all made him want to throw up. Or was it down to the fact that he had not had breakfast? But then again, breakfast wasn't for unemployed graduates. He looked down at his papers again.

Diamond Marketing Consultancy needs a Marketing Manager. Qualifications - HND or BSc in Business Management or Marketing. Desirable - at least three years managerial experience.

Then a deep rumbling voice yelled from the back and interrupted his thoughts. It was getting closer.

'Repent of your ways! Many of you are taking bribes, stealing and accumulating wealth. Do you not know that money is the root of all evil?'

Bayo closed his eyes.

'If these people are going to disturb our peace, at least get the scriptures right,' Miss Pink Suit and Sunglasses commented.

Bayo looked up and saw the man coming towards them holding a big Bible. He stood in front of them, his eyes set firmly on Miss Pink Suit and Sunglasses.

'You sister, have you given your life to Christ? Will you be ready when He comes back?'

The woman pinned her gaze on the deep-voiced young man. 'My relationship with God is my own business and for the record, the scripture you are quoting is wrong.'

'What do you mean?' He scratched his head, clearly not used to being challenged.

'Go and learn your Bible well. It says the love of money is the root of all evil, not money itself. First Timothy six verse ten. Was it not money you used to pay your fare on this bus?' A few people clapped.

'Don't mind these religious folks.' It was the market woman who was, to Bayo's dismay, still eating the smelly eggs. 'They come in here screaming at us as if we were heathens. My father is a lay preacher in the Anglican Church you know. I was quoting Bible verses from the womb.'

An old man laughed. 'Preacherman, if you are looking for people taking bribes, stealing and accumulating wealth you are looking in the wrong place. Even the policemen can't afford the fare. If we had money we wouldn't be on this stinking bus, would we?'

More laughter as the bus finally moved for the first time in forty minutes. The wind from the sea blew into the bus, cooling the temperature and tempers. The conductor apologised to the big lady for asking her to pay twice, and to the police for asking them to pay at all. The preacher sat down and read his Bible and was replaced by a trader selling a potion that he said cured every disease.

'You see this medicine,' he held up a bottle of a suspicious green substance, 'it cures everything from hiccups to HIV and we are selling it today and today only for ten naira!'

'Really?' A few sceptics weren't impressed.

'It is 1998 and you people still believe in all this nonsense,' said a university student, shaking his head. 'It's probably just dirty water.'

An old woman sighed. 'These things work sometimes you know. Can it cure this bad back?' She looked up at the medicine seller.

'Yes Madam. It is made from specially brewed herbs.'

'Which herbs?' asked the old woman.

'Sorry I can't tell you that. It's a special recipe.'

'Are you sure it isn't something you pulled up from your backyard?'

The trader hit his chest. 'I can't lie. I go to church every Sunday. Ask that man at the back there. He bought some last week. It cured his eczema.'

People turned around to see the man at the back that had stood up and was nodding his head.

'It's true. This medicine really works. See my face.'

Another man shrugged. 'How do we know that you aren't the man's accomplice. Both of you could be trying to con hard-working people like us out of the little money we have.'

Other passengers agreed with this. The trader, seeing he was losing ground, pointed to the back of the bus. 'See that Madam at the back. I sold her some last week. It was for her husband. He was having private problems.'

Someone laughed. 'Ha! Problems with his privates and this married woman chose to tell you instead of the doctor. Are you sure you aren't having an affair with this woman?' More laughter.

Bayo found himself laughing and decided to put the papers away in his briefcase. It was impossible to read in this atmosphere, especially as they were now heading towards Lagos Island.

Ten minutes later, the bus rolled into Nnamdi Azikwe Street in Idumota. Bayo and Miss Pink Suit and Sunglasses got down and stared at each other as the crowds jostled past.

'Come, I will buy something and get your change.'

She shook her head. 'Don't worry about it.'

Bayo looked embarrassed. 'No, it won't take a minute. I want to give you your money.'

She shrugged. 'It's up to you. I thought you had an interview to go to.'

He stared at her. 'How did you know?'

'Who else would be trying to cram the history and statement of accounts of a company into their head, in a noisy bus?'

He sighed. 'I really need this job.'

'I pray you get it.'

'Thanks.' He stood there looking at her, torn between his desire to pursue his romantic inclinations and his need for a job.

'What time is your interview?' She looked at her watch.

'Eleven am.'

'It's almost eleven.'

'Good-bye then.' He stammered as he glanced at his watch and turned to leave.

'Tell me how it went.' He turned around and she flashed a smile. A small one, but it was a smile. 'Maybe I will see you at the bus-stop again.'

Bayo smiled and nodded.

THREE

THE GUEST

℘

Moisture was everywhere. And just like the little beads of water running down the walls of the front room, rivulets of sweat ran down my face into my mouth making me want to spit. Mildew formed dark spots on the carpet. My sleeveless linen blouse and blue jeans offered little protection as they stuck to my skin.

The door opened.

He wore a clean white vest and *sokoto* - loose trousers made from traditional cotton print. My father walked slowly now and was much thinner. His hair was totally white, but his eyes remained youthful pools of light that searched mine for answers.

Your mother was dying. Why didn't you come?

'You look just like your mum.' He lowered himself into a chair.

I had to swallow back another chunk of the past and feel it slide from my tongue down into the pit of my stomach, making me wince like a child after it had swallowed bitter medicine. I knelt to greet him.

23

'Good afternoon Father.'

'Welcome back.'

He held out his right hand and I took it, noting how hot it was. Aunt Lizzy came in, on cue, and pressed a cool glass of water into my hands. My father and I chatted about my work as a lawyer. We touched on the weather and the current state of the British monarchy, which I knew he maintained a keen interest in since his days as a student in England. Then I stopped, having run out of any more words to fill in the gap that years apart had widened.

In my head, I heard the very last conversation I had with him. Words had oozed out of me like poison from a festering boil. He had stood there with his new bride and told me to shut up, but I had carried my mother's burden for far too long. Now, all that needed to be said, had to be said. When I had finished, the room was silent, except for my mother's tears.

℘

I stared at the cause of all my problems. The first day I had gone to my father's office and saw her fawning over him I should have known. Her type was guaranteed trouble, always looking for some marriage to wreck. Tall, slim and in her late twenties, Tolani had bleached every bit of what was noble and memorable out of her face, leaving this taut, unnaturally orange-grey image garnished with eyebrows that looked like question marks. Think of a fruit that has been left out too long in the sun. That sums up my father's former wife. A gold-digger endowed with an enormous bosom and tiny waist, she was a magnet for men in the throes of a mid-life crisis like my father was.

He had stood up, the veins standing out in his neck, his voice cutting into me like the whip he used on us when we were children. If I didn't like life in his house, I could leave, he had said. My mother pleaded for him to reconsider but I was already upstairs throwing my stuff into a suitcase. He reminded me as I walked out, that if I stepped outside his house I would no longer be his daughter. That suited me just fine. I was eighteen at the time and I had endured enough of him. He was the commanding officer and his family were the recruits he had trained to obey his every directive.

I stayed at my best friend's and two weeks later mother came and gave me a one-way ticket to London out of her 'rainy-day' account.

'Your father will not be pleased, but the house is not good for you now. It is better you go back to 'your' country.' She tried to laugh but there were tears in her eyes. 'Do not forget us in Nigeria.'

'Of course not Mum. I can't forget you.'

I had left her to pick up the pieces.

When I arrived in London I wanted to put it all away. I loved my mother and my young brother Kunle, but as I grew into my twenties, I had to explore what life had to offer.

Although Nigeria, with all its problems, was just six hours away by air, I was light years away from the place. I didn't bother to visit so of course, I had no idea about the illness until Kunle rang to tell me. By that time it was very serious. She had forbidden anyone to talk to me about it - being a nurse, she knew how bad it was. Typical Mother. She didn't want me to worry.

ℰꙅ

'Sit down. You must be tired after your journey.'

His red-rimmed eyes followed mine as I looked around the room taking in the broken, worn chairs and the dirty carpet. When I'd left, it had been soft and plush under my feet, but now the golden-brown opulence had turned to the shade of coffee, stiffly brushing against my open-toed sandals. There was a sofa I didn't recognise but even that was threadbare. In the corner was a cabinet with some forlorn pieces of china and my mother's hourglass timer. I remembered how we used to shake that timer and watch the golden specks pass from one chamber into the next. I gently eased myself into one of the chairs that looked the sturdiest and stared at the cabinet again.

He kept looking at me. 'Another mistake of mine. After I lost the government contract, Tolani left. She also took my son and most of your mother's china.'

'How is he?'

'Fine I suppose. He is nine now and costing me a fortune like his money-grabbing mother.' He got up and unlocked the middle shelf. 'She didn't get this though.' He handed me a small box.

The box held some golden trinkets and a gold necklace, stuff I remember my mother wearing. I blinked back to thirteen long years ago, and saw her standing at Departures, waving until I disappeared.

'Your mother wanted you to have it.'

'Thank you.'

His lips twisted into a smile as he looked at me, hard, for a long time, as if he wanted to remember me after I returned to England. 'She would have been so happy to see you here. Why didn't you come to see her when she was ill?'

'I was afraid. Kunle told me what the sickness had done to her.'

'What does it matter now?' He rubbed his eyes. 'I went to my doctor yesterday you know. He gave me some medication. I don't understand it. It makes my eyes water like that of a woman.'

I remained silent. The man I knew never cried. My brother told me that when they were burying Mother, he sat through the funeral despite the wails and screams and sung 'Abide with Me' with eyes as dry as hot sand.

'Dr Ajayi knows his stuff. Been my doctor for some years now. He is running tests on me because they say I am not eating. It's total nonsense but he is a good doctor.

Trained in America you know. A big hospital in Boston. He was very good when your mother fell ill...,' his voice trailed away, then he coughed. 'Well what can we do about what God proposes?'

Aunt Lizzy returned with a covered tray and as she placed it on the table, I realised how hungry I was. My father excused himself and shuffled to the door, his movements slow and laboured. I caught sight of the hourglass again, a constant reminder of my childhood. It stood proudly in the cupboard with my mother's plates – the ones that came out when we had guests.

I picked up the hourglass and shook it. Aunt Lizzy watched me.

'I remember how you and Kunle used to play with that thing when you were kids.' We both watched the golden sand flow out of the top glass chamber to the bottom.

'We do not know how many rainy seasons your father has left.' She lowered her voice, just for me.

I noticed the sand was now cascading down into the bottom chamber.

'See the bottom chamber? That's where a lot of his days have gone. Make the best of this visit. He cares about you. He is so proud of what you and your brother have become.'

The door opened and Father shuffled in. 'All this talk talk. Let the girl eat Lizzy! You can tell her about all the family gossip later. Enitan, sit and eat some real food.

Better than all that stuff pumped full of chemicals you eat in England.'

I sat down and took the cover off the plate revealing hot curried rice, chicken stew, plantain and black-eyed beans. 'I can't finish all this.'

'Try,' Father and Aunt Lizzy urged in unison.

I put the spoon in my mouth and savoured my first spoonful. I heard Aunt Lizzy ask Father whether she could bring him some food and he said he was OK. Something rose in my throat and found its way out of one eye, dropping unceremoniously as a tear into my plate where it was soaked up by the rice and stew.

Somehow, in some weird way, the scene touched me. To see this helpless old man. To remember the good times. To remember my mother. I pushed the food to the other side of the plate.

'Eat and stop playing with the food. That's why you are so thin. Is that what the men over there like? Women as thin as mosquitoes?' She rolled her eyes. 'You should eat more so that the men can see you better.' She patted her posterior and laughed.

Father coughed again and looked to us for support. 'Which brings us to the matter at hand – have you managed to find yourself a good man yet?'

'Dad…I'm too busy for all that.' *I only just turned thirty for goodness sake.*

Aunt Lizzy suddenly made an announcement. 'Papa. Our guest has just arrived.'

There was a knock on the door and a young man walked in with a confident bounce. He was a bit taller than me, wore glasses and looked in his mid-to-late thirties. He greeted me warmly and I nodded in his direction not sure about this familiarity from a man I did not know. There was a hint of an accent - American - but with some Nigerian flavour mixed in somewhere. His clothes were casual yet smart. Expensive labels too. I could tell. I know Nigerians did not do dinner in casual dress. That was the kind of thing you did when you had lived abroad for some time. I looked down at my jeans and sandals.

'Lizzy go and bring more food for our guest.' My father's voice was stronger, the lines of sorrow on his face now erased and his eyes brighter as he turned to me. 'Enitan meet *Dr* Dayo Ajayi.' Emphasis on the *Dr*.

I gave him one of my plastic smiles. 'Hi *Dr* Ajayi.'

The man did not look surprised at my underwhelmed response to his title. 'Nice to meet you Enitan.'

As his hand swallowed mine up in a handshake, I noticed that he had a pleasant smile and that apart from the glasses, he wasn't bad looking at all. This visit was turning out to be less painstaking than I had thought it would be.

FOUR

The Taste of Home

℘

The event was taking place in a modest two-bedroomed house on Paradise Street, a row of brick houses battered by time and the last war. This part of East End London had been badly defaced by Hitler's bombs and now two decades later, the sense of abandonment and gloom hung in the air like the early morning smog.

Oyedeji was excited. He had been waiting all week for this party and from the looks on the faces of the people around him – he wasn't the only one. He couldn't believe there were so many Nigerians in this area. The celebrant was a Nigerian doctor from a rich family. His father was some big military man back home. No wonder this chap could afford to spend lavishly on his second son's naming ceremony.

Oyedeji was particularly enthusiastic about the food. And here, there was lots of it - good home cooked *Moi-Moi*, jollof rice, fried chicken and fish and assorted alcoholic beverages. He had not eaten this well for a long time.

'Good food eh?'

He looked up and saw a sprightly gentleman who had been holding court in the sitting room. He had merry, knowing eyes and a face lined with years of experience and rejection. His unnaturally black hair contrasted with his white eyebrows. His name was Mr Coker, but everybody knew him as Baba London - and Baba London knew everybody. The stories about him were many. He had fought in the Great War. Others said it was the Second World War, during which time he helped the British fight Hitler. Baba London was what some Nigerians scornfully referred to in those days as an 'eternal student' – one of those unfortunate fellows who had failed to pass their exams over and over and was doomed to roam the streets of London until he was white-haired and toothless. It was better to do that than go home to face the disappointment of family and friends because you returned without any qualifications. It was the '60s and Nigeria needed professionals to go home and build up the civil service the British had put in place.

Oyedeji nodded at Baba London as he tucked into his plate of jollof rice. 'Great food. It is good to meet people from home.'

Baba London agreed. 'Listen to me my son. When you are in a foreign place like this, it is good to stick close to your people.'

Oyedeji smiled and watched as a pretty, young woman came up and gave Baba London a plate of food, curtseying as she did so.

'That is my wife, you know.'

Oyedeji nodded politely. How did an old goat like this manage to get his hoofs on such a pretty girl? The old man followed his gaze and chuckled.

'Listen my friend. If you have a bit of money, you can marry the most beautiful girl in Nigeria. Are you married?'

Oyedeji looked incredulous. 'I am not even earning enough to look after myself, let alone another person.'

'Well, when you have saved up enough money, ask your people back home to send you a good wife.'

The young woman returned with a glass of water, curtsied again and left. The old man's eyes followed her greedily. Oyedeji's lips curled in distaste. What was it about these old men and their insatiable desire for young flesh? He looked at the young woman and gave her a wry smile. The poor girl probably cooked for him, kept his home neat and tidy and submitted herself to his intermittent clumsy advances in return for the chance to live in England and send money home to her family. He turned back to Baba London and watched him as he attacked the fried chicken with his brown, stained sharp teeth.

'Whatever you do, do not marry a white woman. They will make you look down on your culture and your people. Your children will grow up not knowing your family.' He beckoned to his wife who brought him a beer.

He remembered Sandra, the English girl whose number he had taken a few weeks ago. He still had not called her. His flatmates had discouraged him from doing so.

We don't want trouble from the neighbours, so you better steer clear of oyibo girls. You know what happened to so and so.

Mr Coker had not finished. 'You may think I am an old man but listen to this old man. There is wisdom in white hair. I have been in this country for almost forty years now and I can tell you that those kinds of marriages never work. I used to work with one chap from Ekiti in the western part of Nigeria. He married this white woman. One day he cooked cow foot and she saw him giving some to their little son. The ignorant woman went to social services and said the man was trying to force the boy to swallow a bone. Then when such people want to go back home, the white woman threatens to keep the children behind. When it comes to marriage, home is best.'

At some point, the old man started to sing a song and people gathered around and sang with him. The wistfulness on their faces and longing in their voices ushered in a sad and melancholy air to what was meant to be a joyful occasion.

> '*Home my home*
> *Home my home oooh*
> *When shall I see my home?*
> *When shall I see my native land?*
> *I will never forget my home*'

Suddenly bored, Oyedeji picked up a can of beer and watched a young lady walk past with a tray of *akara*, a delicacy made from fried beans that made his mouth water with longing.

'Could I have some of that please?' he smiled at her politely.

She stopped and gave him a plate. His eyes swept over her taking in the neatly plaited hair - a pleasant sight as most of the women in the room were wearing wigs – and the simple *buba* and wrapper, a blouse teamed with a long strip of patterned material she had tied around her slim waist. Her eyes were large and deep set in a dark face, her smile revealed a gap between her teeth and the two small tribal marks on her face told him that she came from Abeokuta, a large town in western Nigeria.

'Thank you.'

She smiled and moved on gracefully through the crowd. He watched her go, his eyes fixed on her posterior. He smiled slowly then turned his attention back to his food. Nice looking but a little plain. He simply liked his women the way he liked his food, spicy like this *Moi-Moi*. His eyes flicked through the crowd and settled on another girl. She was fair with bright pink lips the same colour as the silk blouse and skirt that showed off some ample cleavage. Her hair was swept up into an elaborate beehive. He held his gaze until the girl looked up and gave him a small smile.

∞

The summer nights lengthened into autumn and he found himself working a collection of assorted jobs. At that particular moment in time, he was a cleaner in a care home and a security guard in a firm that made electrical supplies.

Slush swept away the debris summer had left behind and the streets were now slippery. Oyedeji fell down a couple of times trying to walk fast like the *oyibos* who had been born with the ability to walk like robots, in all kinds of weather. And so they should be able to – it was their country after all.

It was on one of these cold, wet miserable mornings, whilst standing at the bus stop, that he remembered the attractive *oyibo* girl with a man's laugh. Sandra. Her number was still hidden away in his suitcase under the warm clothes he had brought from home. You never knew when you might need such things - warm clothes or a warm-hearted white woman.

ℰ𝒪

His security job meant he worked late and her work meant Sandra would pop into the offices after everyone had gone home. Sometimes she would bring a take-away and a couple of beers. On one such evening, she was sitting on her uncle's chair eating fish and chips and asked the dreaded question.

'You got a girlfriend back home Deejee?'

'No.' He remembered Elizabeth, the student teacher waiting patiently for him back in Lagos and realised that he was no longer the same person she had fallen in love with.

'What about a wife? I hear you folk usually have three or four wives, like a kind of harem.'

He put down the bottle of beer, smiled and decided to humour her. 'Yes. In fact, my father had eight of them.'

She choked on the food and swigged her beer. 'Eight?!'

'Maybe nine. I forget.'

Silence. Then a cough. 'So how do you do it then…I mean, keep all those women happy?'

He shrugged. 'I wouldn't know. I have never been married to several women at the same time.'

'Yeah I know, but I'm sure you and your mates talk about these things.'

He was deep in concentration, shovelling the mountain of mashed potato and chicken stew into his mouth. Mashed potato was a poor substitute for pounded yam, but he did not have the money to buy food from the African food shop. All he could do was eat and pretend it was the real thing. She coughed again making him look up. He didn't know why he covered up the food and wiped his hands on a piece of tissue.

'Deejee. Why are you eating with your hands like that?' Her mouth was open.

He shrugged. 'That's how we eat our food back home.'

'You're not back home Deejee. You're in bloomin' London!'

'So what? Whatever part of the world he finds himself, an African man is an African man.'

'I dunno. It just looks so…'

'So what?'

'It's not sanitary.'

'The British want to lecture me about cleanliness? This is a country where warm water comes at the touch of a tap, yet you people build your bathrooms outside in your gardens and bath once a week. I come from a country where people walk for miles to bathe in rivers, every morning.'

He watched Sandra go red.

'Sometimes I don't know why I bother with you. What did I say that was so bad anyhow?'

He did not look up from his food. 'Sandra, do I complain when you eat fish and chips with your fingers?

She played with a strand of her hair. 'Don't be silly Deejee. Everyone eats fish and chips with their fingers.'

'You know this for a fact eh? You have looked into everyone's house and seen them eating their evening meal with their fingers?' He returned to his bowl of food and continued eating, sucking on a chicken bone.

Sandra closed her eyes. 'I can't believe you are eating a bone.'

'That is the sweetest part of the chicken. You get all the juices.'

She looked at him with distaste. 'You know what Deejee?'

What was it now?

'Have you ever thought of changing your name?'

The muscles in Oyedeji's neck tightened. 'Why would I want to change my name? My father gave it to me for a purpose.' He finished the food and covered the plate, washing his fingers in the side bowl on the table.

Sandra got up and manoeuvred herself into his lap. He sat there unmoved. 'I was thinking the other night when you told me about your problems getting a job as a trainee accountant, and I said to myself that if you had an English name and could try and change the way you speak…well… people would say…well he's almost British and give you a chance.'

Oyedeji sighed. 'I could speak like the Prime Minister and it would not change the colour of my skin. Besides I don't have the time to go for elocution classes. I am not Eliza Doolittle in 'My Fair Lady'. If people cannot take me as I am…,' he shrugged.

They looked at each other and were both silent.

She lifted her lips to his. 'I like you the way you are.'

He looked into her eyes and smiled.

෴

It was Oyedeji's first Christmas and the cold that pierced his soul made him long for the land of his birth. Here it was all about giving gifts, so the shops were full of merchandise and everyone went into this shopping frenzy. Sandra took him up to Oxford Circus to see some pop star switch on the lights. It was an enlightening time, not because he saw how quickly the frugality of the British disappeared during the month of December, but because it was the first time they had gone anywhere together in public.

Maybe it was the beer they had shared in a little pub in Soho that made them this confident, but by the time they got out of Mile End Station, they were holding hands while she lay her head on his shoulder. As they exchanged a long kiss, he felt someone hit him hard on the side of his head. He broke away and looked back at the sea of cold, hard, white faces, mostly of the working-class variety, spilling out of the tube.

'Ooh, what was that?' Sandra looked a bit scared.

Oyedeji shook his head and they moved on through the crowd down the road. Maybe someone had hit him by mistake.

They crossed over the road, laughing and whispering to each other as they continued down the alley to her street. He was focussed on kissing her again, so he did not hear the footsteps but he did hear the curses rushing at him, followed by the first blow.

He did not know how many they were. Their heads were bald like babies, but they had fists that pounded into his ribs and feet that kicked at his stomach and head until he gagged up the steak and kidney pie he had washed down with a beer. Just before he thought he was going to die, he saw his father's face, shaking his head at him in pity. He thought he could see disappointment on the man's face.

Is this your studies eh? Is this what you have come to do in London? An oyibo woman for goodness sake?

He saw Sandra's face loom over him like a picture flickering in and out of focus. She was screaming and crying. Then someone kicked him again and he floated away to wake up in a room full of bright lights with this woman with black stains running from her eyes pulling at him.

ℰↃ

'He's awake.'

The tall man in the white coat spoke so quietly that he could hardly hear him. He caught the words though. Concussion…broken ribs. He closed his eyes because it hurt to keep them open.

ℰↃ

The next day a nurse came along to dress his wounds. She brought along a student nurse to observe her ministrations. Oyedeji's eyes narrowed with recognition as the student nurse's eyes met his. It was the girl from the party who had served him *akara*. The plain one with the kind eyes. A needle grazed his arm and he hardly felt it before he drifted off to sleep.

She came back to see him later in the afternoon. Her hair was packed into a white cap and she wore her blue striped uniform topped with a white apron that was as crisp as her manner. The tribal marks on her face stood out like exclamation marks on her young face. She was silent as she checked his temperature.

He groaned. 'Come to say I told you so have you? I deserve to be here, lying on this bed in pain? Go on say it.'

She shook her head. 'I saw her when they brought you in. Why do men like to look for trouble?'

Oyedeji tried to laugh but stopped because it hurt so much. 'What's your name? My name is Oyedeji.'

Her lips loosened into a smile and he saw the gap in her teeth which he now found curiously appealing. 'It's Beatrice. Beatrice Adigun.' She looked around and bent over him to straighten the covers. 'I can't stay because if Matron sees me talking to you for too long, l will get into trouble.'

He returned the smile and whispered. 'A nurse. I'm impressed.'

'I was sent to this country to study and that is what I have come to do. Maybe you should focus on your studies instead of chasing white women.'

His eyes closed. 'I knew it. You people can never mind your own business. I have the right go out with whomever I like without being beaten to a pulp. I thought this was meant to be a bloody civilised country.'

Beatrice was contrite. 'I'm sorry. I didn't mean to….'

He sighed. 'It's ok. I am a bit tired.'

'I will come and check on you tomorrow.'

'What? And kill me with your nagging?'

She shook her head and as she headed towards the door, she heard him groan again.

'Are you ok?'

'If you do decide to come tomorrow, try and smuggle some proper food in before I die in this place.'

'That would really get me in hot soup.' She shook her head. 'I will come to see you tomorrow.'

'I will look forward to it. Thanks Beatrice. You are very kind.'

She turned around, left the room and went to the next patient, leaving Oyedeji to close his eyes. For the first time in days, he smiled.

FIVE

A Very Serious Matter

ɛ⌒ɔ

'Maybe you need to sit down Ma?'

I stare at the tall, young policeman. He has two tribal marks that run down his face like big, black tears but his voice is gentle. I think he is new in this job. I am sinking. The room is spinning around me. The policeman tries to calm me down as I prostrate myself across the blackened tiles of the police station's floor, hands on my head as I rock back and forth silently, like someone in mourning. People are staring at me but I do not care.

Later on, when they sit me in a chair I let myself think of you. You were such a beautiful baby. A contented child that grew into an intelligent student. Such an obedient and God-fearing daughter. Yesterday, I had dreams of becoming the proud mother of a doctor, saturating myself in the glory of having given birth to a child of such supreme intelligence. Voices would lower in respect when I approached. That is Mama Doctor. People would mention their ailments to me at parties and I would tell them not to worry as you would diagnose their problem.

Today my dream died.

The accident on the Lagos Ibadan Expressway had caused a terrible go-slow. It stretched for miles, like a multi-coloured ribbon of cars. My fingers clench tightly around the clasp of my handbag until they ache. The pain does not help. The policeman says that the car was unrecognisable. That you both had to be pulled out. 'Madam, there was blood everywhere,' he says.

The car was headed for Lagos, two suitcases in the boot. They show me your pink overnight bag and point to another much larger one. Smooth black leather with the initials TW. It is the kind of suitcase that a man would carry. He has been taken to the hospital too.

Security men in black suits are around and they lead us to a room. They ask us questions we cannot answer. They are joined by another man. A big man whose large, drooping belly strains against a jacket weighed down by medals and commendations. He keeps shaking his head at us, as if we know more than we are telling him. The security men leave and are replaced by a policeman.

'An important man has been shot and is fighting for his life. Your daughter is found lying beside him in the car. I find out that she recently purchased a jeep with his card. His bank book was found in her bag along with her driver's licence.'

I stare at the superintendent's heavy jowls. They are shaking now, along with his head as he pounds the desk. I am shaking too, with disbelief.

You don't even know how to drive.

He turns to your father. 'Mr Oni. I am sure you understand the seriousness of this matter. I need you to co-operate and tell me everything you know.'

Your father sighs. 'We have brought our child up as a studious, hardworking and God-fearing young lady. I am perplexed myself as to what has happened here. She came home a few weeks ago.' He puts his head in his hands. 'I don't know. I just don't understand.'

The superintendent points upstairs. 'My boss, the *Oga pata* at the top, and the secret service people want me to send you people to Alagbon CID, pending further enquiries. This is a matter of national security. What do you want me to tell him?'

Your father throws his hands up in defeat, showing his palms. 'Our hands are clean. We know nothing. We are just ordinary folk.'

The superintendent signals to his sergeant, a small man whose uniform is several sizes too big for him. 'Sergeant Innocent! Go and bring the case.'

Sergeant Innocent, whose duty is to uphold the law and treat all suspects fairly until judgement is passed, turns out to be not so innocent. He has already judged and sentenced you. I can see it in the twist of his lips as he scurries to his boss' side like an obedient child.

'Yes Sah! Which case Sah?'

His boss seems to glow from within. His eyes bulge out of his head. 'The case that your mother brought here! What kind of a question is that? The case of the suspect of course.'

'Sorry Sah.' Innocent bows himself out of the room.

Silence swallows us up and as we wait, I hear steps echoing on the cold concrete floor. He comes back with your pink travel bag, which he presents with a dramatic flourish then opens slowly, like a magician with a box of wonders and tricks, ready to tempt the imagination.

'Open it.' The superintendent is waiting, eyes on our faces, as if they will reveal the information our mouths refuse to deliver.

Innocent now quickly opens the bag and brings out a red bra covered in black lace and matching panties with most of the area that is supposed to cover a woman's decency missing. It was as if a rat had chewed at it. Any hope I have that this is a nightmare that will end the minute I wake up dies a quick and brutal death. I remember the story I learnt in my secondary school days about a woman called Pandora, who against advice, opened a box that brought calamity upon the world. Innocence runs his hands over the clean neatly folded skinny jeans that I bought for you the last time I travelled to New York. His fingers linger over the silk of a short, red dress.

The quiet in the room is deafening.

The superintendent turns to your father. 'Are these the clothes of a studious, hardworking and God-fearing young lady?'

Innocent is restless. 'We also have more evidence. Many photos.'

The Superintendent gives him a warning glance. 'OK. Get on with it. We didn't come here to sleep.'

My lips are shaking. My destiny is gone, and the roof over my home is exposed to the vultures who will tear us to pieces. Your father lowers his head and I realise that I am your only champion in this room. So, I speak. 'What do the clothes in this bag have to do with the accident?'

The superintendent leans towards me, as if he is sharing a secret that he doesn't want my husband to hear. 'We are hoping you can tell us, Madam.'

'We have told you all we know.'

The sergeant hands his boss a small, black phone and he taps some buttons. 'We have managed to open this phone and retrieve the messages.'

Darling Toye. I love you and I can't wait till we meet again.

He scrolls, his eyes squinting at the screen.

See you this weekend. Love you. Told my parents am studying this weekend and can't come home. Let's meet up. Last night was...

He looks up at us. 'There are more here, but out of respect for you both, I will not read them out. There are also a lot of explicit photos of your daughter.'

My mouth opens at the same time as your father storms out of the room.

'Shall I go and bring him back?' Innocent, eager to prove his efficiency, is looking expectantly at his boss, who shakes his head.

My sigh weighs a lot. It is full of memories, regrets. There is anger too.

How could you do this to me?

'How long was this going on Mrs Oni? We have reason to believe that she might have been used as bait by enemies of the senator. Her accounts show regular large deposits from a company which we believe is linked to him.'

'I tell you. I don't know anything.'

The superintendent sighs. 'That may be the case, but you have to understand my problem. I have a case to solve. You tell me that you know nothing about this, but I find it hard to believe, Madam, that you really thought your daughter was as innocent as you think. It is good that your husband has gone, so we can speak frankly. You see I am a father, a parent too.'

Innocent coughs loudly. He is scratching his head. 'What about this *Oga*?'

The superintendent shakes his head, but it is too late to stop the sergeant from bringing out a small packet adorned with heart shapes and waving it in the air. I stand up and tie my scarf around my head. My mouth is too dry to talk and my heart too broken to cry. 'Since you are a parent Sir, you must understand why I need to go to the hospital.'

The superintendent's voice seems quieter. 'Sergeant. I think we have finished this interview for the moment. You can turn off the tape now.'

'Yes Sah.'

'I would like to continue with this interview tomorrow though. You and your husband are free to go to the hospital now. We will however send officers to accompany you.'

I nod at him as he walks out past the policeman on the counter who jumps up to attention and salutes. Sergeant Innocent, having singlehandedly redefined innocence, follows with the big, black suitcase in one hand and the small, pink one in the other. Their footsteps echo on the cold concrete floor.

ℰℴ

Your father is silent as he stares out of the window. Even our driver, a generally talkative character, is remarkably reticent. I try to dredge up memories of a conversation we had the last time you came home to Lagos. You were glowing with youth and energy, slim and pretty in your usual outfit of t-shirt and slacks, telling me how busy you were at university and how you were looking forward to our holiday abroad. It was going to be your first trip to London. We had made plans together; we were going to have this big graduation party in a couple of years to celebrate your first degree. Then it would be more years in medical school.

How did you know this man? Where was he taking you? You told me you were studying this weekend? What made you leave your campus?

I have no answers. Only questions.

ℰℐ

Your father gives me his back as he continues to stare out of the window, even though there is nothing new to see along the long stretch of road leading to the hospital. Eventually we get there. It is a simple two storey building with several cars parked outside. There are more security men rushing around on their phones. One of them blocks the entrance wanting to know my name and why I am here.

'I want to see my daughter.' My voice is determined and louder than usual as I tell him your name. I catch the look of embarrassment on your father's face as he wipes sweat from his brow with the sleeve of his *dashiki* top. Reluctantly, the security man steps aside to let me in. We get to reception and I repeat my request. The receptionist hardly looks up.

'What is her name Madam?'

One of the security men whispers something. She stares at me, her lips half open and shiny with cheap, bright, pink lipstick. I wonder whether she has a hearing impediment, so I repeat myself again – this time louder and in my native language.

'*Omo mi da?*' - Where is my child?

She gives me a cold look. 'I do understand English, Madam.'

I put my hands on my hips and stare back. She picks up the phone, says something then continues writing without looking up.

'Doctor is very busy. Can you take a seat?'

We sleepwalk in the direction of some plastic chairs arranged in a row. There are about ten people waiting to be seen. One is an old woman, another a young man with his arm in a plaster, behind him a pregnant woman, next to her an older man with a little girl who looks to be about three years old. She is smiling at me. She reminds me of you when you were a little girl…a long time ago. I ignore her. Your father tells me to sit down on the chair next to her.

'I will stand.' I start to pace the floor, head down, mouth working in furious prayer.

'Suit yourself.'

Your father sits down heavily and stares at nothing in front of him, as if in a trance. It takes more prayer and another forty minutes for a doctor, a young man in a white coat, to come down the stairs. His tone is direct and business-like as he speaks with us. His professional detachment leaves me even more bewildered. Immediately, I burst into tears.

It's my fault. I am the Mother. Even my own husband blames me.

Your father and the doctor continue their discussion in low, hushed voices and I interrupt them.

'Where have you put her? I want to see my daughter.'

The doctor nods. 'They are just getting things ready Madam. I will go upstairs and see if the nurses have finished.'

'What are they doing to her?'

The two men exchange glances. I feel your father's hand on my shoulder. The doctor leaves.

'Evelyn...'

I look at him. The man hasn't called me by name for years. Not even during our most tender moments. I want to say something but the words that form in my mind get stuck in my throat on the way up to my mouth. On top of that, the scent of disinfectant sears through my nostrils. Then, a loud scream rips through my thoughts. It is coming from one of the wards upstairs.

A woman is cursing you and your generations yet unborn. She does so in our language which makes the words even more potent, piercing my flesh through to the inner marrow of my soul. Curses and more curses, loud and foul, fill up the spaces in my head that are not occupied by questions, pain and betrayal. Shame burns me up.

A nurse beckons and I draw as much courage as I can into my heart and command my reluctant feet to move. I enter first. Your father stays outside while I close the door behind me and stare at you as you lay there, so still and silent.

෨

I don't know how long I have been sitting here crying. These tears just will not stop. The voices outside are closing in on us. I hear the woman's sobs followed by your father's quiet voice trying to calm and reassure. Then more words. They question our capabilities as parents. They say that we did not train you properly and that you are nothing better than a prostitute, a home-wrecker and that you deserve what has happened to you. I watch you through my tears as you lie on the bed, your beautiful eyes closed, unaware of the drama unfolding around you. A story in which you now play the leading role in the final chapter.

I begin to pray again, my mouth moving feverishly as I recite the Lord's Prayer. Familiar, calming words in my unfamiliar world.

Our Father who art in Heaven...

Then silence. The shouting stops, and your father comes in. We look at each other again, then a small voice calls my name and I see you open your eyes.

'Mama?'

'Yes, Sade. We are here.'

Your eyes struggle as you search my face for rejection or censure. I have no time for either. Your arm is attached to a drip and your left leg is bandaged and attached to a hoist.

'Mama. My leg hurts.'

'Papa Sade. Can you get the nurse? Our daughter has returned to us. She needs some pain relief.'

He doesn't move. 'Ask your daughter what she was doing in that car?'

I lower my voice into a whisper. 'Now is not the time. Let us thank God she is alive.'

'Look at all this disgrace she has brought to the family. Then there is her brother at the bank and the other at school. How can they hold their heads high in the middle of this scandal!'

'Papa Sade! Sssh.' I look to see if you can hear us and see tears trickle down your beautiful face as you try to speak.

Your father paces the room as he does when he is in the courtroom. 'This is a very serious matter. Look at all this *wahala*! We have policemen and secret service downstairs wanting to know what you were doing in that car! For goodness sake – we all thought you were safely in school!'

Sade's voice was weak. 'They came out from a junction and started pursuing us, firing bullets. I was scared. I begged him to drive faster. Then we hit something, and I can't remember anything after that ...'

'Somebody! Get the nurse!' A voice shouts from outside the room.

Your grip tightens on my hand as the door flies open and a woman rushes in. A policeman follows her. Then suddenly her hands are on you, slapping and hitting any part of your body that is not attached to some medical device. I stare at her in horror before my maternal instincts kick in and I pull her away. She is in her late thirties. I recognise her from the newspapers and TV. Today she is without make up, jewellery or elegant clothes. Her simple, loose African kaftan doesn't disguise that she is at least five months pregnant.

Shola Williams isn't speaking with the well-modulated English accent she uses when campaigning with her husband, singing sweet but empty promises of a better life for ordinary Nigerians. Nor was she cooing as she does when posing for photographs next to big-bellied children with dull brown hair and dry skin. Her eyes are lifeless, yet her chest is heaving with emotion as she faces you.

'He is dead! Are you happy now?! You can go and tell the people that sent you that the assignment is over!'

I stand over your bed. 'We are so sorry for your loss, but our daughter is innocent of any complicity in this.'

Shola faces you and folds her arms across her chest making her belly protrude further. 'So *Sisi Eko*! What happened eh?'

'A car came out from a junction and started firing bullets. Then we crashed and I don't remember anything else.'

Your father is shaking his head. 'Madam. Let the police handle this matter. Interrogating my daughter is against her rights and it achieves nothing.'

'How could the bullets miss her eh? It is only because she was sent by his detractors. It's all part of a plot! You dare talk to me about rights? What about my husband's rights? What of the rights of my children to a father?'

I shake my head. 'I am so sorry for this unfortunate, terrible thing that has happened to the senator. I pray they catch those responsible but I have no idea how this happened. This is not my daughter's fault. They were driving and three men in a black car opened fire on them. She was hurt herself.' I see a hint of pity in her eyes.

'Did you know about this affair?'

I am silent.

Shola laughs. 'So, she didn't tell you. If she could lie to you about what she has been doing with my husband for the past year, then she could lie to the police and to all of us! Don't you see?'

'Madam…please.' Your father tries to speak.

She hardly looks at him. 'I don't have business with you.'

She wags her finger at you. You lay there with your eyes just staring into space, as if you are in another world while we are left here fighting and shouting.

'So what was it?! You stupid little harlot? What did he promise you eh? Money? Maybe a trip abroad? They say that what a man loves most will kill him one day and now it has happened. I used to warn him, but no, he would not listen. He thought I was just jealous. He had everything and he gave it up for what?' She hisses. 'You have made innocent children orphans! Yes, the two at home and the one in my belly. I curse you and everything you will ever be in life, that is if you have a life after this. The police will be up to take you away soon and I hope you rot in prison. I will personally make sure of it!'

Then she walks out and slams the door.

You burst into tears. I want to comfort you, but I see the look in your father's eyes and decide that now might not be the right time. I should have disciplined you more, made you study harder and not let you go to parties or allowed you to have boyfriends. I am the Mother. I am to blame. He is just the Father. Childrearing is my department. Your success is his achievement. Your failure is my responsibility.

'I'm going home. You can stay here with that disgrace you call your child if you like!'

His words are cold as he slams the door. I hold you in my arms. Now we can cry together in peace.

ℰↃ

It's hard to imagine that it has been a year since this very serious matter began. It is said that everything must come to an end, but not this business of the senator. Sometimes I wonder if it ever will end.

The late Senator Toye Williams was a rising star in Nigerian politics and was expected to run for the position of president. His loss was keenly felt during the recent presidential election. I do not know or understand how you managed to get involved with him. Even though this matter has uncovered sides to you that I still don't understand, I must continue to love you. It took a long time for me to gather all my courage together and ask you why you were having an affair with a man almost twice your age. I knew I had to do it if I was going to totally forgive you. I told you I needed to know the truth.

I regret it now.

ॐ

It was about six months after the accident.

You sighed, and it was as if it took all your strength to answer me.

'I loved him, Mum.'

I realised then that you were not the same girl I used to drag to church every Sunday morning and evening. 'But he was a married man,' I pleaded.

'He was the only man who really understood me. I never had to get distinctions to be loved. He was kind and very generous. Had a great sense of humour too. He told me

I had the most beautiful smile in the world. He used to call me his 'First Lady in Training'. He would hold me like...'

I covered my ears. 'Stop it! Stop it! I don't want to hear any more of this nonsense. You didn't go into this willingly. Tell me he deceived you, forced you, took advantage of your youth and inexperience.'

You went on, your voice cold and emotionless. 'Mum I'm an adult. Nobody forced me. I wanted his baby you know. He was the one who was worried about my studies and what my family would think. He told me he was going to leave that witch and I believed him. Then I got pregnant and he made me have an abortion. Then a month later, I find out from the gossip papers that he is to become a father again! At 50! I can still see the headline, 'Senator Toye and Shola Williams at the Achievers' Ball'. Shola resplendent in a blue ballgown showing off her baby bump. It was all in the news. That was the day I promised to take my revenge. He thought he could continue to use me and play happy families?! No way!'

I think that is when I collapsed. All I can remember about that dreadful night is that I could not feel my hands and feet, nor could I speak. If it wasn't for your medical knowledge, I would have joined our ancestors by now. Sometimes I wish I had.

Anyway. A mother's love is like the sea. You can never tell where it begins or where it will end.

୫ᴑ

Now all you have to remind you of that love affair is a limp in your left leg. There is also the reality that your older brother Rotimi will never forgive you for causing him to miss out on being promoted to bank manager. His bosses did not want the publicity of hiring one of your relatives.

Things are a bit better now that the police have informed us that you've been cleared of any involvement in the assassination. For once in my life, I am happy at their ineptitude. Rotimi has a job in a smaller bank and your younger brother no longer has to hear all those horrible things said about you at his school. I cannot believe that secondary school boys can be so crude and wicked.

I must take things very slowly now. Ever since that dreadful night you revealed all and I had the mini-stroke, I try not to let things get to me anymore. It is not easy, but what can I do? Your father introduced me to a very good doctor who is monitoring my condition and he says I will live long enough to see my children's children.

Anyway, it is good that you are in London now. Your father and I both decided that the one year's compulsory National Youth Service was not an option. Anyway, I think it is better for you to finish off your medical training abroad. Just as well we had some savings. I believe that your love for medicine will give you a good future, one that will not let the past become a regular visitor in our lives.

ℰℭ

Your father has decided to marry again. At first, I was so hurt and disappointed. During the last year when I needed his support the most, he was often away on business. Now I realise what kind of business it was. I realise that everyone has ways of coping with a crisis. I turned to church and he turned to women.

She is a very young woman. Lola is her name and she is about your age, 26. Very pretty and very intelligent. She is in her final year at university where she is studying law. I carry no malice for him or the girl. My load is heavy enough and hatred will make it even harder to bear.

How things have changed. When I was a young woman, all I wanted to do was go to university, but I just about acquired a few 'O' Levels before marriage and motherhood were decided for me. Your father would not allow me to go back to school while you were all young and as you got older the dream simply faded. I had to content myself with reading as many books as I could find to better myself and increase my proficiency in the English language so as not to shame your father. He had a very important job as a lawyer and I made it my duty to ensure that he would always be proud of me when we had guests.

So many opportunities for the young women of today and yet you all squander it away. Now your father's new wife is putting me through the same hell that the senator's wife suffered. I pray that you will never again be the source of another woman's suffering, another fatherless child's pain.

ᔕᑎ

My daughter, I love you enough to want better things for you. You see, a mother's love is a very serious matter. It is like the sea. You can never tell where it begins, and you will never know where it ends, because it has no ending.

One day, when you become a mother, you will understand. It is a very serious matter.

SIX

GREEN EYES AND AN OLD PHOTO

ॐ

He was embarrassed as he looked at the black and white photograph. I took it from him and realised that it had been torn into two. It was a picture of a young couple, a black man and a white woman with red hair and green eyes like mine, standing in Trafalgar Square amongst loads of tourists and pigeons. They were smiling.

Then a woman in her mid-fifties wearing an expensively embroidered blouse and skirt came into the sitting room. She was small, dark and looked like someone whose life had been good to her. She looked content. Until she saw me. At that moment, her eyes glowed with resentment and jealousy. Her footsteps quickened, and she moved to the front door.

'Baba Jide. I'm going out to see Mrs. Johnson.'

He shook his head and sighed as the door slammed behind her. He turned his attention back to the photograph.

'I took it about a couple of weeks after I met her. I was still trying to come to terms with England. My first few minutes in the place and I thought the cold winds were going to snatch my heart out of my chest. Nothing I had heard or read had prepared me for it. My favourite books on England eulogised about log fires and crimson-cheeked families drinking wine and eating lots of meat whilst singing hearty choruses. No book told you how cold it was - a cold that went deep into parts a thousand jumpers and heavy coats could not keep out.' He chuckled to himself.

'I could not complain because it was my desire to study abroad and join the ever-growing ranks of the new breed of African, the ones who had bagged the 'golden fleece' - a British or American education. Sometimes when the cold was especially biting I would think about how one day I would go back to Nigeria with my qualifications and make my father, a retired accountant in the civil service, proud of me.'

'Remember the family you come from son. Do us proud'. Those were the words of the old man as he stood at Apapa Docks, eyes red. My sister was there too, shedding tears as if I was never coming back. I was the only boy out of three children and my mother had been too upset at the departure of her only son to accompany us. Her last words were a tearful admonition 'Make us proud'. The awesome sense of responsibility to achieve great destiny had been impressed upon me and I could not fail, for to fail spelt family disgrace.'

෨

That first morning in Portsmouth, after my first sharp catch of English air, my eyes struggled to adjust to the grey and bleak shadows in the morning light on the dock. As the ship got nearer, I realised that those shadows were people. I had no idea how I was going to survive in this climate.

It was another cold day when I met your mother. I remember because I was wearing this cheap coat I had picked up in Petticoat Lane. The material was useless - like paper - and I was freezing. I think I had been in the country for about two months by then. As I had done every morning for those two months, I was walking down the road on my way to the Labour Exchange in search of a job. They were standing outside the pub – four, maybe five of them. They were tall and thin in the black jeans and shiny leather jackets they wore, their greasy hair slicked down with side partings and heavy side burns. I could smell their fear lurking beneath the stink of cheap alcohol as they hurled insults in my direction. That was the first day I heard that word, the 'n' word. Bitter. Full of contempt. Spat out like their phlegm hardening on the pavement in front of me.

I thought to myself. See these ignorant people? They can't think of any other word with 'n'. I wanted to show them that I knew more than them, that 'n' was for Nigeria, the land of my birth, and Lord Nelson, who won the battle of Trafalgar and died in such a dramatic fashion with one arm, faithful to the end, and that there was another Nelson, currently imprisoned on Robben Island in South Africa for expecting equal rights in the country of his birth. Hatred burned out of their opaque eyes as they surrounded me like a pack of jackals, spitting and snapping.

'Hey monkey boy? What you gonna do? Wanna fight?' The one who seemed to have a problem with his salivary glands swaggered further towards me. The others stood behind him, wise enough to be scared of this unknown African. They wanted to see my tail. At that precise moment, I wished I had one so I could tie it around their necks and watch them choke. They thought I was a savage, an animal, but I was a gentleman. They were the animals, pure scum. I decided that I would not give them the satisfaction of a public brawl. I politely tried to make my way past them, but they blocked me. I was outnumbered. I tried again.

'I would appreciate it if you could kindly let me pass?'

Their eyes popped out of their heads, like freshly caught shrimps.

'Oooh. It speaks posh,' said one.

'Oiii...you leave 'im alone!'

I looked up and saw a young woman approach. Young, with a hairstyle that looked like a mass of shiny copper coins done into a high contraption on her head. She was wearing a short pink coat and a white dress with a huge white belt and matching white boots. I looked past her to the boys, confident that I had the height and the physique to deal with all of them.

She stood in front of me, put a hand on my arm, and shook her head. 'Go on love. They aren't worth it. You touch them, and you'll just get banged up because the bobbies aren't going to listen to a word you say.'

I did not know what getting 'banged up' meant, but I did realise that if there was a fight it would be my word against theirs, and I did not think the word of a black man would count against the word of these pasty creatures.

One of them shouted again. 'Blackie! Why don't you clear off and go back to your country and live in your trees?'

I saw the woman put her hands on her hips. 'Why don't you all clear off and go find some decent work to do for a change?'

They sniggered amongst themselves and made some rude gestures with their hands warning me that if they ever saw me around the area again they would panel beat my face. I wanted to stay and show them that I was a man, then decided that I would rather be a free man than one locked up in prison in another man's country.

I decided to keep walking. So deep in thought was I of the eccentricities of the English, that I did not hear the footsteps behind me. Expecting trouble, I turned around and saw the same woman that was now a beautiful, young thing. She had the longest eyelashes I had ever seen on any woman and her eyes were green. Green was good. Green, white and green. The colour of the new Nigerian flag.

Green, the colour of the bush that surrounded the gates of our compound in Lagos. Home.

'You showed 'em.' She put her hands on her hips and laughed.

I immediately found her very refreshing. This was the first English person that I had spoken to in the two months I had been in the country, and one that had not cursed, grunted, or compared me to some form of wildlife. I smiled even though I could not recall showing those impolite fellows anything, but I liked her laugh. I had never heard a laugh like that. It was like a man's - deep and confident.

'You look as if you're a long way from home.'

I put my head down and continued walking. 'This is my home for now.'

She ran to keep up with me. 'Slow down mate. I'm only trying to be friendly.'

I reduced my pace and looked at her again, remembering the stories I had heard about the sorry ends of black men who were friendly with white women. My knowledge of this was mostly gained from reading magazines like Jet and Ebony at the American consulate in Lagos. Mr Jim Crow and his brothers were not allowed in England. Here everyone was equal. I remembered my sixth form tutor Mr Reginald Smith reassuring me as a student, 'You see in England there is no segregation. We pride ourselves on our fairness and equity.'

He hadn't lied about that. It was evident on my street where both white and black lived united in mutual poverty squashed together in the little boxes they called houses. England was truly a country where people lived as equals. A place where a black man could exchange smiles and conversation on a street with a white woman, without being hassled. I was impressed.

She smiled at me. 'My name's Tina.'

I could hardly understand what she was saying but I did get her name. I took her hand and shook it, bending my head slightly forward in respect as I had been taught to do when meeting a lady - the benefits of a public-school education... African-style.

'Oooh...you're a real gentleman. We don't get many around 'ere. So what's your name then?' She giggled.

'Olu. I'm a student from Nigeria.'

She looked a bit confused. 'Is that anywhere near Jamaica? There's a girl where I work who is West Indian... but you sound so different.'

'That is because I am from Nigeria.'

'Where's that then?'

'It's in Africa.'

Her eyes widened. 'Africa? You must have lions and tigers running around in your backyard all the time then?'

I looked at her and laughed. I laughed because I was talking to a white woman who was not my teacher, the local shopkeeper or my landlady. This was my first light-hearted conversation, even though her ignorance of the western coastal region of Africa was bloody woeful. It was probably on the same level as the colonials who had lived in Nigeria for years though. Nevertheless, something told me that she was a good woman.

Even though I was mesmerised by her sea-green eyes, I had to correct her false impressions of my country. 'We do not have wild animals running around in Lagos. It is the capital of Nigeria. Just like London is the capital of England.'

'You talk posh. Where did you go to school to learn to speak like that?'

'King's College, Lagos.' I stood up a little higher when I said this. I was proud of my Alma Mater and the school motto, 'When the call is sounded, all must answer here'.

The conversation went on. We were both curious about each other. She kept staring at me.

'We don't get that many round' ere like you.'

'Sorry?'

'You what?'

'Around where?'

'Around 'ere? Around these parts. Canning Town. People here don't really like darkies.'

Back in those days you would have had to be blind not to notice the twitching curtains, the hard looks on the street and the whispers of tight-faced housewives as I walked down the street. Every man I met seemed to have a dog as a sidekick and they reminded me of the kind of evil criminals I had read about in the Charles Dickens novels during my time at King's College. They had this evil aura around them. I remember a Ghanaian friend telling me that some dogs had racist tendencies passed down to them by their owners.

As we walked along, the heavens opened, so we ran to the nearest bus shelter. Luckily for us it was empty, so we could continue our conversation without being hassled by anybody.

'So, what's Lagos like then?'

'I can tell you about Lagos. In the afternoon, it is so hot that you feel as if the sun is burning into your skin, and the sweat runs down your body until your clothes stick to you. In the evening, you get a cool breeze coming in from the Atlantic. I used to go with my schoolmates and sit watching the big ships come in from all over the world.'

'Sounds smashing.' She smiled at me.

'Smashing?'

'Yeah. Smashing. Like the Beatles…and Elvis'.

'Smashing,' I repeated it to myself. A new word, a new experience. I liked Elvis though.

'I went to a concert once you know. Girls screaming away like banshees. It was great.'

'Elvis?'

'No. The Beatles.'

We should have long parted ways, onto our separate buses, but we kept on talking, right there under the shelter until other people arrived. We were oblivious to the disapproving glances of middle-aged women, local troublemakers looking for fights – essentially, the entire world around us. I went home that day with a number in my pocket, a spring in my step and a smile on my lips.

ℂ

'I called your mum a week later. I wasn't too sure she would answer my call, but she did, and we arranged to go see a film. I think it was one of the James Bond movies. We started seeing each other, albeit tentatively, because she feared her family finding out. They were the kind of people that believed Africans lived in trees and had tails. About eight months later, you showed up and we decided to get married.'

'We both loved The Beatles and played their music at our wedding reception. Small thing. Just about 10 people, mostly students really. That was the song 'She loves me yeah, yeah, yeah'. It was just the four of us at the Registry. Two of my friends and two witnesses - my landlord and a kind stranger off the street. Her family didn't want anything to do with it.'

'I used to have quite a few photographs of the wedding that I had locked away in my study, but my wife is always spring cleaning. You know how it is like with you women. She said she doesn't like me to dwell on the past and threw a lot of them out. Sometimes I like to look at them - just to remember how things used to be.'

℘

I remained silent throughout his monologue. My mother must have meant something to this man for his second wife to resent her so much, more than forty years after her death.

'I am really glad you have come Sarah. I have told your brother Jide all about you. He is at work now but looking forward to seeing you.'

I was curious to meet my younger brother and hoped he was more like his father than his mother.

'Maybe tomorrow I can arrange for us to go to Ikorodu.'

'Where is that?'

'Our ancestral home town. It is a small town just outside Lagos, where my parents were born. We have a house there and I want to introduce you to your aunts and uncles.'

It felt good to belong. My first time in the country of my forefathers and I truly felt that I was part of something bigger than myself, my two children and my accountant husband, back in faraway Cricklewood, a leafy middle-class suburb in London.

'That would be nice.'

જી

It was later in the evening that I heard the music. It was coming from his study blaring out into the warm night.

> '*She loves you, yeah, yeah, yeah*
> She loves you, yeah, yeah, yeah
> *She loves you, yeah, yeah, yeah, yeah*'

SEVEN

TANIMOLA

&

I watched our houseboy Sam pour the tea into a china cup and ruminated over the events of the day. The china set was a wedding gift from Mrs D's parents and reminded me of life back home before the war, rationing and bombs became a constant, gloomy reality.

We got married in 1939. It seemed like a lifetime away from the impending wave of horror and destruction that would go on to scar the world. Sometimes I felt a bit guilty when I realised that getting posted abroad had stopped me from being blown to pieces on some forsaken battlefield.

'That's all now...you may go,' I said slowly with the tone and smile I reserved for Sam, the gardener, the driver and the rest of the Nigerian population. Despite the modern-day attitude, I strongly believed in the importance of everyone in each social stratum knowing their proper place. So it was only right that I set the appropriate tone with the workers. Things might be changing back home, but in Africa, the Englishman was still king.

'Tank you Sah,' said Sam bowing and shuffling backwards out of the room.

There had been no children, something that still hurt, but with the life we lived, maybe it was for the best. Africa was a bit like offal - an acquired taste. Some loved it, others hated it. I had been here for several years now and was still trying to get used to the sheer unpredictability of this posting. Sometimes I wondered whether I was mad to take on this job, that of District Commissioner. I really had no choice though as I had been a senior clerk in the Foreign Office making this a jolly good opportunity.

'You'll do well there Deakins,' my boss in London had said. It was either this or the Sudan and this seemed the less painful option.

'A few years out there and you'll be ready for a top job back home,' they'd said.

So, I ended up here in Ire-Akari, an area as big as Manchester, but buried deep in the western part of the colonial protectorate of Nigeria. It was a place full of heathens and contentious natives who were all conspiring to make my life as stressful as possible. It was all Lord Lugard's fault. As colonial ruler, he had merged the northern and southern protectorates of Nigeria into one in 1914. Indirect rule through the indigenous rulers may have worked in the Muslim North, but like many others, I had misgivings about extending it to the South. I remembered the words of my predecessor.

'These Southerners are too wily. Don't trust 'em an inch. Some of them will smile at you and play the fool, then cut your head off the next minute if they had the chance. They resent us taxing and governing them. Give them a little authority and they are levying their own people, confiscating their subjects' wives and livestock and stoking the embers of revolt amongst their people, while all the while pretending to work with us.'

This was good advice that I let guide me in all my dealings with the African, and it had served me well.

I wiped my brow and pulled off my stiff khaki jacket. A lot of those milk-faced fashionable girls that I had considered as a single man would have caught the first boat back to Southampton. Not Mrs D though. She had a good, strong disposition that one. A sensible woman, Mother had said, is what you need and thank God I married one. Mrs D was a treasure. Salt of the earth.

Today I almost sacked Christopher, the office messenger. He was a man of almost two score years with at least three wives I'd heard, which was a feat considering what we paid him. It was a pity that he had the intellect of an infant and the tact of a rhinoceros. He'd only gone and brought in a bunch of people shouting and waving their hands in the air. After we had managed to calm things down a bit, he told me that they were from the palace.

I put on my best smile and asked him to bring out the chairs. Part of my remit here was to keep the local chiefs happy. That way I wouldn't have to deal with riots and villages warring against each other. In my eight years here, three without Mrs D, one thing I had realised about the African was that he was a creature of simple needs. Give him food, women and the chance to dance and worship some deity, and he was as happy as a lark.

The king's officials of state wanted us to come to the palace to deal with a problem. One of the king's *oloris* - wives - the youngest one, had been talking to herself. Well, in fact, they'd said she was talking to spirits. One morning, she had run into the central market…in her birthday suit. As this just wouldn't do, we had to take her with us.

I must confess the thought of the king's wife first made me go all red and pull at my khaki shirt. I had seen her at his side during a state function and she was very beautiful, and very young. I was glad that the fan was blowing hot air around the room, a good cover. Then I started questioning them. Why this drastic action? Could they not send the girl back to her people? I knew this place they wanted to send her to and it was the epitome of bedlam – there was no more chaotic a place on this side of the Atlantic. Mrs D went there with some of the folk from the church as part of her charity work and came back with the most dreadful tales.

Christopher tried to reason with them but there was more shouting and gesticulating and shaking of heads. Apparently, the king wanted her out of town because she carried an evil spirit and had committed an abomination. What this abomination was they refused to say except that it was enough for the king to divorce her and that the madness

was punishment for her sin. They said I could have her if I
wanted; in fact, they were ready to give me what Christopher
said was a fortune - cowries and goats - if I got her out of
the palace. Realising that they could not be entreated, and I,
feeling like Pontius Pilate, called for my clerk and told him to
draft a letter and send a wire to the hospital.

℘

It is the dry season when the *oyibo* woman comes. The last
time she came was during the great rains. She has a big,
black book that she waves in our faces and makes us clap
and sing songs that we don't understand. She is thin that one.
I wonder what her husband holds onto at night. Her skin is
white and dry like fermented cassava and she has a thin line
on her face out of which she speaks with a high, shrill voice
like an angry spirit. She is certainly angry now as she points
at me, shouting at the orderly who comes to give us food.

Instead of the usual watery beans and cassava twice a
day, that make us keep going to the latrine, we have some
rice and a little meat. Well, more bone than meat really, but
after months of eating those beans, my tongue liked it.

James, the hospital orderly that usually beats us, tells
me that the woman is the wife of the Big *Oyibo* in the
Government House and that she wanted to know how I
ended up here. I tell him that the heads of both him and the
oyibo woman are not correct and he picks up the cane. The

white woman restrains him and smiles at me. Maybe it is the smile or maybe it is the fact that there is food in my belly. I cannot say which, but I begin to her tell my story.

℘

I was walking through a forest of shadows and the deeper I went, the louder and louder the sounds got until they swallowed me up. Just at the mouth of the hill, the house appeared, and I saw a tall man by the door, waiting. I reached him, and he pulled me inside, close to his chest. His arms were strong like the branches of a young tree, his touch shutting out the voice of conscience as his fingers slid across my neck.

'What of the sacrifice and the prayers?' I tried to move away but my legs would not carry me.

My lover laughed. 'Save them for later,' he'd said.

I shook my head. 'Alani. Are you serious about helping me with this problem? I am not like those other women that come to see you…'

'Tanimola, sometimes these things take time. You need to trust me. This is the only way the medicine will work properly.'

I glanced through the window, knowing that the darkness would not shield us for much longer. 'I can't wait for long.'

'Neither can I.' He smiled as he let his hands play around with the beads around my neck. 'Why are you trembling?'

I closed my eyes. 'Just be quick and let me get back.'

He laughed, and the night shadows swallowed us up as he turned down his oil lamp and lay down with me. He was a strong man that one. His body firm like an *iroko* – hard redwood tree - his breath hot against me as he whispered my name. I closed my eyes. I remember thinking that maybe he would give me a child. A strong boy.

∽

I was dancing at the yearly harvest on the day the king's officials found me. There had been a good harvest that year and the land had given birth to enough food to fill every hungry mouth. In the sixteen harvests I had known, never had barns been so full of yams and grain. We danced ahead of the older women who let us shine, knowing it was our time for suitors. I was one of the dancing girls, my hair freshly plaited and woven around my head, like a new basket. My arms rose and dipped like the branches of a tree caught in a breeze. Then the drums stopped, and the king's men beckoned to me.

'What is your name?' he asked.

I told him it was Tanimola.

The next day they brought twenty yams, ten sets of new clothes and a hundred cowries of currency to my father, promising another two hundred cowries if I was a virgin. Father got the two hundred cowries after my first night with the king. I became his Number One Wife – the only one whose food he would eat and whose bed he would visit more than the other wives in his compound.

Then my story changed.

One harvest met another harvest, the rainy season was replaced by the dry season and yet the crimson flow did not stop, continually mocking my desire to become a mother. The king's older wives sneered that I had as much chance of retaining his seed as a basket had of keeping water.

℘

One day I found myself walking to Alani's house. The moon hung in the sky lighting the way as I ran through the bushes along the back paths, my feet heavy, the ground beneath dampened by the night rain. I wrapped my cloth tighter around my head as I watched the sun creep out of the morning's mist. I knocked on the door and watched his mouth open as he rubbed his eyes.

'I wasn't expecting you.'

I smiled. 'Alani! When do I need an invitation to visit?'

He blinked. Twice. Like he was…seeing a spirit. 'Yesterday…'

'Yesterday when you saw me in the market I was tired from the sleepless nights, feeding our son.'

He smiled but his eyes were hard, like black stones, just like his heart. 'He is our son now eh? Yesterday morning he was the king's son.'

I smiled. 'I have thought about it. I am not an unreasonable person. The king is old and as you said why choose an old bent tree to lean on when a new one full of sap and energy is much better. I have made my choice.'

I watched the muscles in his neck tighten as he faced me, smiling sheepishly.

'I wasn't really going to tell the king about...'

I pushed my body close to him and felt it tremble. 'I know you will never tell the king.'

'The king would kill you...and the boy.' He sighed and shook his head. He even managed to look mournful.

I looked at the sky and knew that I had to be quick. 'I brought you a gift.' I pulled out a little bottle from my bag.

His eyes brightened. 'Palm wine?'

I smiled. 'Yes.'

He looked uncertain for a second and I pressed closer to him again. 'Drink it and afterwards I will stay with you.'

He snatched it from me and put it to his lips, laughing as he took a generous sip. Only a little was needed. He had told me himself, one night as we lay together, talking about life.

Then he stared at me. All I could see was the whites of his eyes.

'You have killed me!' He gagged, thick blood mixed with a white, bulbous substance bubbled down his chin, the muscles in his neck now standing out like the roots of the big tree in front of his house. He sank to the floor and tried to reach for me. I shifted away to pick up the bottle, moved to the door and watched him curse and call me every name under the sun, as he writhed and spat like a wild dog. When it was silent, I crept out of the house and headed back to my son and the king. I remembered to close the door so that his clients would think he had gone on one of his long journeys.

He was a very clever man, knowing what herbs to mix and what sacrifices to make to call rain down when it did not want to show its face, what potions could kill and what potions gave life. He knew how to make a woman want him so much that she forgot the meaning of shame, but he was ignorant about the power of a mother's love.

ℰↄ

Back at the palace, I walked into my bedchamber and saw Alani sitting on my bed next to our son and my knees buckled.

The maid asked me what was wrong, but I just shook my head and dismissed her.

He was dead. I had administered the fatal blow.

How could he be standing in front of me laughing with his bloody mouth? Telling me that we are joined for life in the spirit world and that I would never know the joy of raising my son.

ℰↄ

I tried to keep the boy. I tried so hard. It was the fever that took him.

It was during the rainy season, so they had to dig very deep.

I hear him calling me from the future. I hear him calling me from my dreams. In my sleep. When I eat. When I…

છ⌒

That last night with the king, Alani was there. I could smell him. His laugh echoed around the bedchamber as the king gathered me close. He wanted to comfort me. The boy had gone. It was the will of the ancestors. It was our night. He had been eagerly anticipating this more than the nights with the other *oloris*. Had he offended me in any way? He would give me his kingdom. I should smile and look lively in his presence.

I don't want your stupid kingdom. I want my son.

So I lay down with him. Alani was in the shadows chuckling as I fulfilled my obligations.

That night I dreamt that Alani was standing in front of his house in the bush. He was holding the boy in his arms. The boy was calling for his mother. He was calling for me.

The next morning I got up and left the palace. Just like that. I ran towards my boy. I ran into the darkness of the bush. That's all I remember. Then they brought me here – to live like an animal.

No respect. They don't even know that I am a Queen.

ℰ

Richard Deakins went into the little side room he used as a study. He liked to call it a study, but, in reality, it was just a room with a writing bureau, an armchair, a bookshelf and a little cupboard. The bookshelf was stuffed with the complete works of Dickens and Bronte and a stack of pre-war copies of Tatler. The cupboard was partly-filled with bottles of whisky and wine.

He wriggled about on the chair, trying to make himself comfortable, but it was impossible as there was something hard under the cushion. He pulled out an embroidered notebook. Last time he had seen it, Mrs D was writing about the social and cultural practices of the African from the western region of Nigeria. Even Sam had been interested. He had turned to Mrs D.

'Madam wetin you dey write?'

'I'm writing a book.'

Sam smiled. 'Maybe I could read it one day.'

I remember Mrs D's eyes meeting mine. It was one of those many occasions where we shared an amusing moment about the antics of the native people. Sam had not finished primary school but was always staring at a dog-eared copy of the Bible.

'I think this story of the Chief's wife 'Tanimoola' should go into my book,' quipped Mrs D. 'Under the customs and practices of the Yoruba.'

Sam's face darkened as he gesticulated the sign of the cross and backed out of the room.

EIGHT

MEETING THE FAMILY

ℰℴ

The house was in Ungwar Rimi in the government reservation area of Kaduna, a large city in northern Nigeria. It was a large, colonial-style villa whose cream walls and stone-washed pillars rose from the hills. Its spacious French windows opened onto a well-trimmed front lawn hedged by rows of hibiscus, jacaranda, bougainvillea and African roses, punctuated with palm trees.

A young woman opened the front door. Behind her was an impressive, large sitting room with all cream walls, burnt brown and gold settees and chairs and tan velvet drapes. Expensive paintings and carvings hung from the walls and a large cream and gold rug lay on the floor. A pair of huge doors at the far end of the room opened onto the rear garden.

The woman was short and generously proportioned with large, piercing and very beautiful eyes. Her royal purple brocade kaftan fell to the floor in elegant folds and her hair had been plaited into a long pony tail. The expression on her face spoilt the beautiful canvas. It was petulant and dissatisfied. Bola instinctively knew that this was Halima, the Chief's new wife.

Her lips tightened when she saw Bola then relaxed into a smile when she looked past her to Tunde.

'Hello Brother Tunde.'

Bola stood and watched as the woman launched herself at her fiancé.

'Halie. How now? How body?'

'I am fine.'

Tunde turned and pulled Bola to his side. 'Halie. I want you to meet Bola. My fiancé.'

Halie threw a glance in her direction and Bola was conscious of the acute appraisal as Halie summed her up from her hair, her new skirt and blouse, her golden sandals and matching bag. Her lips curled as if she had been sucking on a lemon all her life.

'Really.' She led the way into the house. 'The Chief has been expecting you. I will get Rekiya to serve lunch.'

Tunde smiled. 'So where is Dad anyway?'

'He is in the other annex, having a meeting with some business associates. Let me call Peter to show you to your room. You might want to rest before lunch.'

As soon as the bags were in their room, they went down to eat, after which Tunde gave Bola a tour of the house. There was a pool, a tennis court and several expensive cars lined up on an expansive driveway. The grounds were majestic. Bola wondered if this is what the Garden of Eden might have looked like.

Back in their room, Bola realised that that they were in one annexe of the house that had three bedrooms, all en-suite. Tunde's father lived in another annexe with his new wife. The décor here was total opulence. The last time she had tread on a carpet as soft and luxurious as this was in the Hilton in Abuja. The room had wallpaper - pale green and gold - that matched the rich green and gold tapestry curtains and bed sheets.

'This place is fantastic.'

She felt a pair of strong arms go around her waist and shook her head.

'Tunde! Your father is downstairs.'

He laughed as he whispered into her ears. 'My father is in the other part of the house.'

Bola pushed him away gently. 'I don't think Halima likes me.'

'You've only been here five minutes and you are so sure about that?'

'I saw her face Tunde. A woman knows these things. She hardly said a word to me during lunch.'

'Do you really think I want to be discussing my dad's new wife with you at this point in time?' He looked down at her, raising her face to his, looking deep into her eyes.

'She looks quite young.'

'I think she's about 22 now.'

'That makes her a year younger than me.'

Tunde shrugged. 'That's the way of the world.'

'I hate it. My dad has girlfriends too. Some of them are much younger than me.'

Tunde didn't hear a word as his eyes travelled all over Bola. She had changed into a long green and purple patterned African dress with gold trimming around the neck. It had thin straps and skimmed over her slim curves as it fell to her feet.

'I dunno. I think something snapped in him after Mother left. Maybe it's a middle-age crisis thing. Maybe he is just the typical Naija man. I don't know. I can't answer for him.'

He saw the worry in her eyes. 'Relax. Polygamy isn't hereditary. I'm definitely a one-woman man.'

She glowed in the warm gaze of his admiration but pulled herself away from him and looked at herself in the mirror. The light picked up the dazzle of her diamond earrings, a present he had bought for her during a business trip to Florence. She loved his compliments, the generous gifts, the surprises, the way he looked at her as if he couldn't wait to have her all to himself. She saw his eyes and knew what he was thinking and shook her head. 'Your father is expecting us for a chat at seven, prompt!'

'Dad looked very impressed during lunch. He leaned over and whispered, 'You got a good one there son'. My dad isn't easily impressed.'

'I'm glad. I want your dad to like me.

Tunde leaned in for a kiss.

∞

After meeting with the Chief, Bola felt sleepy and so decided to go up to bed leaving her fiancé to talk with his father. She was making her way up the stairs when she heard someone hiss her name. She turned, looked down and saw that it was Halima. The woman stood at the foot of the stairs, her hands akimbo, her lips stretched into a half-mocking, speculative smile.

'*Wifey* eh?'

Bola stared at her, bewildered.

'You will not last.'

Bola came down the stairs slowly, her face just as hard as Halima's. 'The words of a jealous woman. Why can't you be happy for me? I have not come to fight you.'

The girl laughed, shook her head and disappeared back into the sitting room to join the men. Bola struggled to sleep that night.

∞

The following morning, just before breakfast, she mentioned the exchange on the stairs to Tunde, but he laughed it off.

'That's Halie for you. The girl is a real joker.'

'I didn't find it funny.'

'Halie is just a bit protective over me.'

'Protective or jealous?'

His answer was to snatch her into his arms and bury his head in her neck. 'Now who is jealous?'

'Tunde!'

'OK. I admit I flirted with her a bit before she married my Dad.'

Bola stiffened and moved back. 'Were you guys…?'

His eyes darted from hers and she turned away and continued her packing. That said it all. Then she heard him whisper.

'Come on Bola. I do have a past. You are my future though.'

She closed her eyes as she felt his arms go around her, drawing her in as she fought back the tears.

NINE

WITH LOVE FROM TUSCANY

ℰꙄ

Silence hung heavy in the air between them. He spoke first, his little eyes like that of a rodent, blinking in the heat.

'Ese. Is this you?'

She brushed past him into the coolness of the house.

'Godwin, do I have a twin? Could you not even come and welcome me at the airport?'

He stood up and sat back down again. Then he tried to light a cigar but his movements were shaky, and it took several attempts before smoke was billowing around his face.

'Did you not get my message? I was going to come and then I received a phone call from Lagos and got delayed. It was my older brother. He was rushed to hospital. I had to make some calls to ensure money was in the account to pay the hospital bill.'

She folded her arms across her chest and looked at him. He scratched his head.

'You know our people. They always bombard me with their requests. I try my best to help them when I can.'

'It is well. You didn't tell me you had got a job.'

His voice was softer. 'No. I am trying but it is not easy around here.' He got up and took her suitcase, dragging it behind him.

'It is good that I have been sending money then. I mean how else would your family survive?'

He was silent. Silent like the air around them. His eyes shifted. The last time she had seen his eyes set at that angle he had forgotten to tell her that his mother was coming to spend a month with them. She noticed his shirt. New, like his newly-acquired pot belly. The furniture in the living room, also brand new.

'One suitcase. That is amazing for a woman. Did you get me those leather shoes I asked for and the perfumes for my mother?'

'What of all the ones I have been sending? You people could have opened a shop with all the gold, leather shoes and designer clothes I have sent home in the past few years.'

She curled her lips in disgust. Her money. Her blood. Her life poured out as a sacrifice for people who did not care for her. She was just an instrument to be used for their advancement. Emptied of her vitality, until she was a dry and empty husk. He saw her face and sobered.

'So, you are not joking? You actually came home empty-handed?'

'Godwin, you haven't even offered me water and all you can do is ask about shoes and perfumes! You haven't seen me in three years. Anybody would think that your love for me disappeared the moment I put my foot inside that plane.'

His smile was contrite. 'Sorry. Don't frown like that. You know my love for you is as strong as ever. *Haba*. Don't be angry with me Ese my love. Sit down. Make yourself at home. Let me get you a nice cold drink.'

'Water is enough.'

She closed her eyes and sat motionlessly on the new and richly embroidered three-seater settee until he came back and handed her a glass of cold water. Tentatively, she sipped. They spoke. No. He spoke. There was his new business and the new car that sat proudly outside their house. The village had changed since so many of its daughters had started going abroad and sending money home. Italy had to be a very good place because it was so easy to make money there. Maybe one day he would go there just to taste what the place was like. He took her by the hand and led her to the little room at the back of the house.

'Come and see your office.'

She had never imagined they would have a proper kitchen and so her heart skipped a beat at the sight of all the modern appliances in their little house. A fridge, cooker and kitchen unit. Just like big people's houses.

Wasn't that why she had gone to Italy? So they could live like this?

'No more kerosene stove. Gas cooker. Big fridge.'

He opened the fridge and brought out a bottle of Guilder Beer and an orange drink. The fridge was full of assorted bottles of expensive wines and beer. Maybe something in her silence communicated to him because he looked up.

'Let me get you something from the restaurant down the road?'

She shrugged. 'I don't have much appetite nowadays. The doctor has advised me to get more rest.'

'Of course. Of course. Well, welcome home.' He excused himself and went to the toilet. She headed straight to the bedroom.

Bed. Big. New. She opened the wardrobe. There were all his suits, shirts, ties and leather shoes. Some were still wrapped in their packaging. It wasn't as if he ever went anywhere else but to the beer parlour and parties. She could not understand why he needed all these clothes. That was when she spotted something peeking from under the bed. A woman's shoe. One shoe. Bright red with a black bow. She wondered where the other shoe was. It was not her shoe, she knew that. It was local and cheap and badly made, and probably belonged to somebody local, cheap and badly behaved. There were so many of them around. They bred like rabbits in this town which was amazing seeing that there were so many empty bellies. She heard his footsteps and kicked the shoe back under the bed.

'See how I have decorated it all nice for you?' He looked at her face, like a child waiting to be praised.

She looked around at the cream walls and new turquoise curtains. The bed had new blue and white covers and matching plain blue pillowcases with 'Sweet Dreams' embroidered in uneven italic letters sewn using sliver thread.

'Thanks.'

He smiled wider, having received his praise, and proceeded to talk about everything yet tell her nothing. Did she know that *okada* motorbikes had now replaced ordinary bicycles? That the nearby oil refinery had stopped recruiting local labourers and contractors and that Mama John's daughter had just left her second husband? Was she aware that his mother had the malaria fever so bad that she had to be rushed to Benin Teaching Hospital where she was put on a drip for two weeks? His voice buzzed around her head like a demented mosquito searching desperately for a way out of a net.

'Are you not happy with this room? Why are you squeezing your face as if your head is hurting you? Are you not well? Shall I go and get some food? Is it true that *oyibo* people eat food with pepper? Did you miss Nigeria at all?'

'Yes. No. Godwin...I'm tired. I want to sleep.'

'Yes of course. Italy is not a village down the road. Get some rest. I will leave you.'

She sensed the relief flooding out of him as he closed the door and proceeded straight to talking on the phone. She imagined that he was telling Miss or Mrs Red Shoe off for leaving evidence under the bed. She felt a strong desire to deliver a mighty slap on the prostitute's cheek.

Prostitute. Mignotta. Prostituta. Puttano.

She closed her eyes and laid her heavy head on the cheap silk pillow, wetting it with tears. Out of the corner of her tear-filled eyes, she saw lizards mating in one of the many cracks in the wall. Maybe her money had not been enough to continue with his 'renovations'.

She closed her eyes. There were no sweet dreams for her. Only nightmares.

ℰↄ

Thirty men a day. Sometimes fifty to pay her Madam ground rent for her loco – her little room. It meant that by the time she had finished paying her bills and sending money and gifts home to her family, she had barely enough for food, toiletries and clothes.

ℰↄ

Now it was her body and soul that needed renovation. Sleep was a shameless flirt, proving elusive as memories buried deep under the surface rose up and rumbled around in her head. Her back started to hurt and she got up, put on some chocolate soufflé powder to brighten her dull face and decided to get dressed and visit her family.

Her parents' house had acquired a new door. It was green. Bright green. It reminded her of a young woman who left three years ago for Italy to work as a nanny.

❧

It was all sorted. The job was there. She would love the children. So well behaved they had said. Money? If she was prepared to work hard, her earning potential was limitless. Empty promises, painting elusive pictures in her head.

❧

Her younger sister Dorcas opened the door and stood like a statue, her mouth open like somebody who had just been slapped. She swallowed down the hurt.

'Dorcas? What now? No greeting for your big sister?'

Dorcas was hesitant. 'Welcome Sister. How are you?'

Dorcas reluctantly ushered her into the newly refurbished parlour where her parents sat, stiff and silent. Her father nodded at her greeting and asked her how long she was staying. She told him she was back for good, to settle down with her husband and start a family. Her mother got up and silently left the room. Father and first daughter looked at each other.

'Papa. Why did you not reply any of my letters? Not return my calls?'

Silence. She saw Dorcas turn to look at her father, but he looked out of the window where the children played on the dusty streets. All she heard was the tick-tock of the big clock echoing in her head. She used to sit watching it whenever she was called in for a telling-off or a caning. Her eyes floated over the faded family pictures on the wall as she heard her father's cough. To her ears, it sounded like the kind of cough a person gives before announcing a person's death.

'There was talk in the village. Your uncle said he was told by one Warri woman that you were selling yourself in Italy.'

Her laugh was strong. She sounded convincing. Even to herself.

'So, you just believe any *fabu*, any lies now eh?'

Dorcas looked shocked. 'Please Sister Ese tell me it is a lie! Please!'

She laughed. She laughed so much that tears poured out of her eyes.

'Where did you think all that money to support you people was coming from?' She spoke louder, bolder. 'Don't tell me you really believed me when I told you I was working as a nanny eh? That Europeans would be ready to pay anyone that kind of money?'

Her mother ran back into the room and put her hands on her head, her feet making strange movements as if she was dancing. Ese watched her in the detached way people do when they are watching a boring drama. She knew it was impossible for a person to dance and cry at the same time,

NINE / WITH LOVE FROM TUSCANY

but she did not have the energy to dry any other tears apart from her own. She pointed at her younger sister, pretty with her freshly-styled hair and a green African-print dress with yellow flowers.

'You Miss Dorcas. If not for my money would you be able to call yourself a fashion designer? I heard that your business is booming now.'

Dorcas could no longer meet her eyes and left the room. It was quiet except for the laughter of children outside. She marvelled at how laughter could sound so full even when bellies were empty but bloated with water. She remembered it now. Her mother's voice was always soft and low as she urged her and her siblings to drink more water with their meal.

Now everybody belly full.

But their bellies were silent.

'So, you people are not even going to offer me water?'

Her father picked up his pipe and inhaled. Bluish-grey smoke obscured his face, so she couldn't see his expression.

'Come back in the evening. Your elder brother will be here. Then we can have a meeting.'

Meeting. 'Meeting about what?'

She noticed that her mother's eyes were red. Red like the shoe under his bed. Red like the special nightie she wore when entertaining her clients.

She rose slowly. 'OK. I understand.'

'Go well o.' Her mother's voice echoed wistfully as Ese headed to the door.

She could feel their eyes burning a hole into the back of her head. A head that throbbed with the pain of betrayal as she walked out of the door. A curtain moved as she walked out of the house. An old man stopped to look at her and shook his head. Even a dog saw her coming and barked incessantly until its owner came out of his house.

℘

When she got back home, he was sitting on the porch. He welcomed her coolly as he fanned himself with an old newspaper.

'Did you see your family?'

She nodded and went back into the house. He did not follow her, deciding to remain under the shade, sweating in his new shirt while continuing to pour the contents of another beer into his round belly.

There was nothing palatable in the house so she had to go to Mama John's house at the end of the road. In the heat of the afternoon sun, her collar rubbed against the rash at the back of her neck. The rash had started from the back of her neck and advanced over the rest of her body like a conquering army. Sweat trickled down from under her curly brown Rhianna-style wig as she passed a group of effusive housewives. One of them had to put the tray of dried fish on her head down, so that she could crane her head as far as she could to get a good look. She was proud of her attire, her dark pink suit complete with gold buttons and matching gold shoes. Gold, Tuscany's other parting gift to her, hung from her ears.

She realised that since she was coming from abroad, it was expected that she look the part, dress up and make some *yanga* - show herself off to the locals. She wanted that sense of satisfaction, albeit fleeting, of watching their mouths gape open in jealous contemplation as they did mental calculations of how much her outfit cost.

'How is abroad?

'You look well. Welcome.'

'You off to church? You look so smart.'

'How is Italy? I see you brought wealth back with you. It is written all over your face.'

She made small talk for some minutes then made her way to Mama John's makeshift 'supamarket'. Her shop, by European standards, was practically meagre. Tins of Bournvita, powdered milk, tinned tomatoes and other provisions sat forlornly on the shelves. A fridge stood in the corner and there was a table outside the shop on which tomatoes and peppers had been arranged in little pyramids. Mama John jumped up when she saw her, which was no mean feat considering her weight.

'*Ese una don land?* How are you my daughter?'

She curtsied in respect. After all, the woman was the same age as her mother.

'I'm fine.'

The woman's eyes met hers. There was compassion there and respect. 'It is good to see you back.'

She smiled. No one had said that since she had returned.

'I want to make small stew for my *Oga*.' She picked up some tins of Geisha fish in tomato sauce, some Maggi cubes, some bell chilli peppers and a packet of imported rice. She pulled out 20 euros from her purse and gave it to the older woman who shook her head. 'Don't worry my child. God knows the truth. You were always my favourite in that family.'

She thanked Mama John and resolved to come back another time and squeeze some money in her hand. Mama John watched her go and shook her head.

'Life is wicked.'

℘

Ese brought in a plate of rice and fish stew and replenished the beer. By the time her husband had finished the fourth bottle he just about managed to stagger to the bedroom where he collapsed on the new, big and comfortable bed. She waited until he was dead asleep before taking off her clothes and laying down beside him. She knew what to do. Was she not a professional?

He groaned. 'What is it woman? I'm trying to sleep.'

She whispered sweet things in his ear and turned down the lamp so he wouldn't see how dry her chest had become, the rash on her back, the hollows in her cheeks and the thighs that were once smooth and plump but now like brittle sticks. But she need not have worried. The alcohol had worked. She felt him relax against her and smiled to herself.

Men. Were they not the same all over the world?

ॐ

He woke up and wondered whether the events of the night had been a dream. She had been...not like the Ese he knew. At one point, he was briefly concerned, but he had been too drunk to stop things from going further. Now in the light of day, reality hit him like a cruel slap in the face. How could he have been so stupid? Surely, he should have been more careful. He should not have drunk that much.

He had rolled over and saw that her side of the bed was empty. He got up and called for her but there was no answer. Then he decided that she might have gone to church for early morning prayers, or maybe to her parents. It didn't make sense to him but women were the most difficult of God's creatures to understand. She had been sullen and uncommunicative all day but come night, full of passion.

He phoned her parents and the rest of her family, but no one had heard from or seen her since the day before. Her family said they were concerned. They were worried about her. She didn't seem herself and although she looked very sophisticated and wore fine clothes she seemed to have lost a lot of weight. A little boy said that he had seen a woman that resembled her disappearing out of Abraki on the back of an *okada* showering him with red sand as it wobbled along the rickety road. She had smiled at him and waved.

The night after she left, Mama John opened her shop and found an envelope containing 1000 euros under her door. There was no note with the money. Soon after, Mama John heard about her departure. She was upset and wished that Ese's own flesh and blood had given her more support, but life had to go on. The next Sunday, she went to give thanksgiving in church and her dance was so vigorous that some thought she might pass out. They did manage to settle her in one of the pews and get her an ice-cold drink and she was fine after that.

Over the next few days, they wondered where she had gone. It didn't take them long to conclude that the shame of living in the village might have proved too much for her and she had gone to Lagos. They did not expect to hear from her for a long time and all-in-all, it seemed a satisfactory conclusion for the family. Lagos was a big city. Anyone who went there always got swallowed up by city life and made infrequent visits back home. She had become an inconvenient embarrassment, one that they wanted to dissociate themselves from. With time, her disappearance became a local mystery. Talk was that she had died in Italy and that it was her spirit that had come back to say its goodbyes to her family.

∞

Everything continued in its usual way. Her father decided to take a new wife because the new business was doing well. Her mother took solace in singing songs from the Methodist Hymnal and attending the local Pentecostal church, praying that he would repent and divorce his new wife. Her older brother Paul withdrew his son from the local primary school and put him in a private school in Sadu where his wife had opened a beer parlour. Her other brother Clément's cement business was doing so well that he relocated to Abuja where the big business was. Months later, he was awarded a Chief's title for his services to the local area. Her sister Dorcas' fashion business continued to boom so much so that she expanded with two more shops in Warri.

∞

He had a traditional wedding to his second wife Agnes, whom he had been seeing before her return. Agnes was a small girl with big ambitions and a love for red shoes. Even though he was twenty years older than her, short, balding and with a very big belly, the money he lavished on her and her family was enough to keep her affections.

It was Agnes who was the first person to realise that something was wrong with him. He seemed to be losing weight by the day. In fact, he was so thin, that if a gust of wind blew, he would be swept away. He was no longer able to strut around town in his nice designer clothes as they were too big for him. Another source of worry was his perpetual cough. He sounded like a second-hand car engine that was only fit for the scrapyard, so Agnes nagged him to make an appointment with the doctor in Sadu.

ℰ𝒪

He was shattered and did not know how his legs managed to carry him out of the doctor's office. He did not go back home to Agnes after the doctor's prognosis. He went straight to her parents and gave them his news. Yes, it was the illness – the *Oga* of illnesses, the Chairman of them all and he had only a few months left. Maybe a year. He wanted them to tell him what he was supposed to tell his wife who was now carrying his child. Her parents did not know what to say.

Dorcas burst into tears. 'What will my customers say if they heard this news? What about my potential in-laws? This is so embarrassing.'

Her mother came running and fell on the floor of the sitting room and started to pray.

Her father picked up his pipe.

No one knew what to say to Godwin.

Later, they phoned round and called for a family meeting. They were good at having family meetings. Clement was in Abuja and was too busy to come. He felt it was really none of the family's business anyway.

'Was Godwin a small boy? Surely, he should have taken care of himself, and as for her it was good she had left the town. Some kinds of shame were too heavy for one family to bear.' Clement was merciless.

Paul, the younger brother who had a bit of a soft spot for his oldest sister felt bad about the way the family had behaved but what could he do? He was only the youngest and besides, he did not know where his big sister was or how to contact her to see how she was. Maybe it was for the best. What kind of life would she have had anyway?

℘

Mama John told everyone who came to her shop that Ese had come back to punish her family for abandoning her when she needed them the most. At one of the Sunday church services, the pastor spoke about the evils of parents sending their daughters abroad to work only to end up being exploited by wicked foreigners.

On another Sunday, a middle-aged woman, Mama Susan, donated one million naira to the church fund to repair the roof the missionaries had put in over a hundred years ago. The pastor was so moved that he prayed for her and her daughter Susan who was working as an au pair in Italy. He also prayed fervently for all the other parents whose children were abroad, working so hard as nannies and domestic workers, ensuring that their families were taken care of properly.

TEN

A PAST AND PRESENT FUTURE

ℰ𝒪

The continuous hum of the air conditioner coupled with a heavy stomach after a meal of well-prepared rice, plantain and beans was making me sleepy. I struggled up to focus on the TV and found CNN so I could find out what was happening back home.

I had left England just as an election was underway and was keen to find out who had won. I prepared myself for another inevitable Labour or Tory win headed by another Prime Minister who had the gift of the gab to convince a weary electorate that their party had the keys to solving the country's economic woes. Then a picture of Big Ben flashed on the screen and I heard the breaking news. The newscaster was experienced but even his face could not hide his shock as he spoke.

'Today the British Peoples Party, the BPP, has won the general election in a landslide victory. It is believed that their win signifies a fight back from voters – a protest against the recession, increased immigration, rising unemployment and the state of the economy. Voters were ripe to fall for the BPP's rhetoric.'

A female journalist appeared. She was black. She was angry. There was an Asian man next to her. He looked scared. Her voice, though professional, was trembling with emotion. 'Today is a sad day for England. The BPP tried in 2010 and got nowhere. The country just wanted to rid itself of the Blair/Brown legacy and move on with the coalition but this time the BPP fought a strategic war. They said it was for hearts and minds. They ditched the Nazism and the overtly racist rhetoric and concentrated on going for middle England, still smarting from the devastation of long-term unemployment and repossessions. Then, they zeroed in on baby boomers and pensioners after the coalition had cut their subsidies, benefits and care homes, forcing many to spend the last years of their lives in unmitigated poverty and suffering.'

'I am, as we speak, no longer a British citizen. I have been told to get ready to go back to Barbados. Who on earth do I know in Barbados? My parents have lived here for fifty years. Reporting for United News, for maybe the last time, this is Keisha Williams.'

I stared at her mouth, my heart a solid lump of congealed fear and horror. The British government had just passed a law which meant that I was no longer welcome in the land of my birth. Anyone whose parents were not born

in Britain before 1920 was not entitled to call themselves
a British citizen. It was stupid. It was one of their election
pledges and I had laughed it off. We had all laughed it off.
They would never get in. In fact, they didn't have a hope in
hell. The Unions would fight it. The Church would fight it.
The Commission for Racial Equality would fight it. England
loved curries, Trevor Macdonald and foreigners, so long as
those foreigners contributed to the economy.

Now the new British government intended to repatriate
all so-called 'non-citizens' to their countries of origin and all
those who were out of the country would not be allowed to
come back in. Spouses or children could stay in England if
they could pass a special test for citizens. The only chance
I had was to go to the British Embassy in Lagos and file an
appeal. I and the millions of others caught in this mess. It
would be an appeal to go back to my life, my children and my
husband in London. No, hang on a minute. Michael and the
children would all be repatriated back here to Lagos.

I rang Michael. He was his usual philosophical self. 'I
know darling. I know it's going to mean a big upheaval but...'

'What?'

He was calm. His tones quiet and measured. Then, he
started, and I wanted to scream at him to stop.

'This might be the best thing for us...for the family.'

'Are you seriously thinking that I would want to stay in
this country with my family? I only came to visit my mum and

already I can't wait to come back. If it's not people queuing for petrol, terrorists setting off bombs or someone trying to bribe you everywhere you turn...'

'England is no longer the place you grew up in. You said it yourself. You can see the despair on people's faces.'

'But it's my home. It's the place I longed for when I was in Naija.'

'You can't pretend any more Tola. It's not been the so-called home you reminisce about for a long time. It's been getting worse each and every year. Besides, it's not as if we don't have a home. We did not just fall from the sky. I don't intend for my children to bury my bones in this cold tomb of a country.'

I swallowed hard. 'I can't talk now. I need to call my manager at work and ask her to keep my job open. I'm sure the British Embassy will sort all this out. I'm British. This can't be happening to me. Once I get things arranged at the Embassy, I will start the appeals process.' My mind was full of a million probabilities, none of them encouraging. 'What are we going to do? What about our house. Our car?'

Michael went on. 'We've got a couple of months to claim money. They have got this scheme called the Repatriation Voucher. You get the equivalent in cash for all your assets in the country. I got the form in the post yesterday.'

'They must be mad! It will never work. Two months? To pack up and leave your own country?'

'It's total chaos over here…the councils, teachers, the National Health Service, London Underground and buses are on strike. Most of their workforce being deported is creating a total disaster. The only people allowed to stay are those who can prove that their parents or grandparents fought in World War I or II!'

'I really can't talk now. I will speak with you later.' I couldn't bear to listen to him making plans to return to Nigeria. I needed to get to the British Embassy.

ॐ

Three months earlier, I was back in my home in East London. It was a two-bed house in what I liked to call the quieter part of Leyton. Every time I walked home after dark, my feet did an involuntary quick-step past the smouldering council estate a few yards away from our front door. I had resolved to nag my husband about moving up North before the kids got into secondary school. My kids going to the same school frequented by the inhabitants of said estate would be my worst nightmare come true.

It was a morning, one just like the other mornings in my marriage. There was a time we didn't even bother to come down for breakfast. Now we can't get downstairs fast enough. The house was warm. I tried not to think of the heating bill as I settled the children down at the dining table. Michael was already seated with a reflective look on his face.

It was his default expression when I was around. He wasn't hungry.

'Are you ill?'

'No.'

I guess he just wasn't hungry then. Neither was Temi, my two-year-old. She dribbled milk from her lips. Small, tiny lips like her father's.

He spoke again. 'I've been doing some thinking…'

'Yeah?' I kept one eye on Temi, who was now blowing milk bubbles, and the other on my seven-year-old son who was fiddling around with his school tie and dark blue blazer. Michael scratched his head which I had learnt after seven years of marriage meant that he was struggling with something.

'What is it?'

'I got another letter today.'

'Um huh…,' I murmured, watching milk splash in the air as my daughter's spoon went flying across the table. I dabbed at the milky drops on her pink cardigan. I didn't have the time to coax her to finish her food. She seemed to sense my irritation as her lower lip trembled in preparation for a tantrum. I looked at my husband and realised that he was gearing himself up to join her.

'Is that all you have to say? Um huh?'

'For goodness sake. What do you want me to say?'

'To show some sort of empathy? Some understanding?'

I wiped the milk from Temi's mouth. I knew what was coming.

'I'm a lawyer…and I'm working as a paralegal. I can't progress without a pupillage and they aren't exactly that easy to get.'

I closed my eyes. 'Michael. We've discussed this.'

He stood up. 'So, you can read my mind now? I haven't even said anything yet.'

'We've been through this before.'

He leant over to whisper in my ear. 'Why don't you take that talent of reading my mind into the bedroom with you?'

I reared back as if he had just slapped me. 'I can't believe you want to talk about this…now…here…in front of the children.'

He stood up. 'Not now? So when? You never want to talk about it.'

'I said not now.' I glanced at my watch. 'I've got to get to work.'

'Yes. I can understand you wanting to get to work when you are a manager in a bank. It's a bit different when you are filed under 'Admin'.'

I picked up my daughter and pulled my son to me. 'I can't talk to you when you are like this. I've got to get the children to school.' I started towards the door.

'Bye-bye Daddy,' the children chorused.

'Tola.' Michael's voice was rough. There was regret buried somewhere in there, but he swallowed it down.

'I've got to go. I can't afford to be late.' I was now holding the door open.

'Tola! Stop and listen to me for once! I have been offered a job in Lagos.'

I stopped then. Turned around even. 'You what?'

'My old boss offered me a job with more money. I have the chance to become partner of the practice. It comes with a house and a car. More prospects, more opportunities. We can get a school for the kids out there. With your qualifications, it won't be difficult for you to get a job.'

'When were you planning on telling me about this?'

'I couldn't say anything. I know you would have dissuaded me. You love this place, but it's not my home.'

'You are such a selfish human being.' I spat out the words.

Michael laughed. It was the laugh of a stranger. 'OK. So it's fine when I come over here and start a new life because I don't want to stand in the way of your advancement. But I'm selfish to want you to do the same for me?' He points a finger at his greying hair. 'Take a good look at me. Tola. I am going to be forty next year, yet I am working as legal assistant barely able to support my children. You are the one earning the most and that helps us break even but how long do you think I can let that continue? You are away working long hours whilst I'm the house husband and I can't do it anymore. I'm going to phone Cyril and accept the job. You can either come with me or stay here with the children. It's your country isn't it? So, it can be your choice.' He stood up and looked at his watch. 'I'm off to work.'

I had never seen him like this before. It was as if he had it all planned out and was going to go ahead with it regardless of my feelings. I shook my head and dragged the children out of the house.

'Mummy are we going to be late?' My son was watching my face.

'If we are, it's your father's fault,' I muttered to myself as I nearly bumped into a balding man who was delivering leaflets. He gave me a funny smile, shoved one in my hand and continued on his merry way to the next house. The neighbours were an Asian family, the parents in their sixties. Proud to be British, hardworking taxpayers like Michael and I. Their son was a pharmacist, their daughter, a lawyer.

We lived in a leafy cul-de-sac. The homes had front gardens. I wasn't much of a gardener, but the neighbours prided themselves in keeping their garden neatly planted with what was now a fusion of lavenders, peonies, primroses, violets, roses and chrysanthemums. Sometimes I watched their grandchildren weaving in and out of the flowers. Now with winter here, things were overgrown and faded, having lost their glorious vibrancy. Just like my marriage. All I could smell was decay.

I saw Steven Losley's vacant stare looming out of the cheap, yellow paper the balding man had handed me. The public face of the BPP mocked me, just like his literature that jumped off the page.

Vote for the BPP in the coming election
England for the English
Save our country from the foreign invasion
Vote for England
Vote BPP

As my grip on the children's hands tightened, I heard the whistling of the balding man, the BPP man, and suddenly, a chill of foreboding seeped into my soul.

'*Always look on the bright side of life*
Ta-ra, ta-ra, ta-ra, ra-ra, ra-ra'

ELEVEN

THE MESSAGE

ॐ

The first clue was the phone message. Short and to the point.

The second clue was the skirt. It was short as well and it didn't sit straight on her waist as skirts are meant to. I had first noticed it when she served breakfast that morning but said nothing. My home was a busy place and I had more important things to think about than my house girl's ill-fitting skirt.

Today the rain was drumming on the kitchen window as I prepared vegetables for the evening stew. The door opened and Peace dragged the shopping in. I heard Kole ask her whether she was alright. I turned around to see her properly for the first time. The skirt was just resting below her waist, under the little protrusion. I went over and pulled her blouse up and had a good look. She struggled a bit and then hung her head. I walked away, sat down and got up again. There was a crash of thunder outside.

'How many months are you?' My voice was very quiet.

'I don't know Ma.'

I picked up an empty pot from the sink. 'You don't understand English any more eh? Do you want me to repeat it in our language? You better speak up before I use this pot to reshape your head.'

The girl kept rolling her eyes around in her small head until they rested on Kole. Then her mouth opened in fear and her hands open as if in a silent prayer. I looked at my husband and he looked away. My heart started to pound.

'Kole! Help me to ask this girl who the father of her baby is.'

He was silent. I ignored him and turned to my housemaid. She looked at the floor then at the door, like a small cornered rat looking for a way to escape.

'Answer me! You useless girl!' I spat out the words. My hands shook with the desire to hit her so hard that I would leave a mark on her that she would show her grandchildren. 'Do you want to go back to your village and live in that hovel with the rest of your ten brothers and sisters?'

She covered her head with her hands, whimpered and cowered away. I walked out of the kitchen to the sitting room and came back with a big, black book which I slammed on the kitchen table. 'You will swear on this Bible and tell me the truth. You will swear on the life of your unborn child!' I heard my husband groan.

'Esther…,' he mumbled, his head resting on his chest. 'I won't let you bring heathen practices into this house. I have defiled it enough. I have sinned.'

'Adulterer!' I hit him hard with my fists. 'Liar! God will punish you for this! Have you no shame? A girl young enough to be your daughter!

'Esther…please forgive me. I am sorry.' He was sweating as he prostrated in front of me. I picked up the Bible and flung it at him.

'You have betrayed everything in that book by touching that child.'

'Mum…'

I shook my head. 'What will people say when they see this small girl walking around town with your baby? Does your mother know? She was always pleading with you to take another wife.'

'Mum!' I felt an insistent hand on my shoulder and I turned to look up into my son's eyes.

Ade was my pride and joy. Our only child. At eighteen, he was getting ready to go to university in the United Kingdom. He had my bright eyes and fair skin and his father's muscular build. We had just finished paying the school fees. He was going to be a doctor.

'What is it?' I tied my wrapper, a piece of expensive lace, securely around my hips.

'It's my baby.'

I sighed and said nothing.

'Mum. Dad was just trying to cover up for me. I told him about it last week.'

Peace was still crying, now louder than before.

'Somebody shut that girl up.'

Kole was facing the garden, his face obscured as he looked outside at the leaves and branches tossing about helplessly in the storm.

I looked up at him. 'Since when?'

'We have been lovers for the past few months.' My son looked past me to his father, then back to me. 'After everyone had gone to bed, when everyone was out, when you thought I was studying for my 'A' Levels. Does it matter?'

I was crying now. 'What will people say?'

'I am so sorry Mum.'

The tears continued until the sky cast long, dark shadows on the walls of the kitchen.

Ade shrugged and got up from his chair. 'I am so sorry you had to go through all this.'

'So am I Ade. We will discuss this tomorrow.'

My son nodded his head and left the room, his footsteps slow and heavy. He didn't look at his father.

℘

The phone had buzzed in my bag, the ringtone insistent, demanding a response. Kole had stood up immediately and shoved his hands in his pockets, searching and searching. I had already seen the fear in his eyes as I pulled out his phone and threw it at him. It had landed on the tiles with a loud crash and split into two.

'She's left a message for you,' I had said quietly.

Silently, with tears falling from his eyes, he had lowered himself to the floor and knelt in front of me.

TWELVE

MOVING FORWARD

℘

Chinwe wiped the sweat out of her eyes and adjusted Baby by jiggling him around on her hips so he would stop crying. All she wanted to do was get this washing finished. One of the women from the yard who was also doing her washing looked a bit concerned.

'That child sounds hungry. Have you fed him?'

Chinwe's mouth moved fast like a child's burning after shoving in hot food, her eyes cold as she met the accusation in the other woman's eyes. 'I've already fed him. He is refusing food.'

The woman shook her head and sighed. 'I have some small bean cake and bread. Maybe he might like that?'

Chinwe put her hands on her hips. 'Are you trying to tell me I don't know what to feed my child?'

The older woman looked at her and shrugged. 'No, I was just trying to help.'

Chinwe lowered her glare and directed it at the large pile of washing in front of her. It was her neighbours' soiled clothes: Mr Johnson's *agbada* - wide-sleeved robe - and trousers, his wife's blouse and skirt, Mama Ezinma's kaftan, some shirts from one of the bachelors in the yard and some trousers from the landlord. With baby now on her back, she bent down and attacked one of the collars.

Baby started to cry again and she whispered to him. 'Ay, ay my child. It is going to be alright. Your daddy will get a job today and we shall be OK again.'

Baby kept on crying and so Chinwe stood up, dried her hands on her faded wrapper, eyed her neighbour and crossed the yard to her room. She took Baby off her back, gently laying him onto the most comfortable part of the bed where the springs wouldn't dig into his soft skin. She felt a warm rush of wind force itself into the airless room. There was going to be a storm soon. The skies were heavy, ready to shed their burden - impatient just like a mother with her child.

Chinwe noted that her son had stopped crying and was watching her with dead eyes that looked like the washing stones she used for her laundry. She picked up the covered bowl of *ogi* - corn porridge - added the last of the carnation milk into it and tried to spoon it into his mouth. He spat it out and turned his head away from the spoon. She gave up. Where was the lively child she had given birth to? This one wanted to be carried all the time. The landlord's wife said he should be walking by now and she should know because she'd had eight of them.

She looked outside at the indigo skies, heard the first rumblings of thunder and ran outside to scoop up the load of dirty laundry. He was cradling his son when she came back in, head bent under her load.

'Lanre. You're back.' Her lips parted into a smile as she greeted her husband while putting the bundle into a corner.

He nodded. 'Unless it's my spirit sitting here.' He laughed and it was like the laugh of her village masquerade during the Yam Festival, harsh and bottomless. She twisted her hands and took a step towards him.

'How did it go?'

'I got to the office, did the interview and afterwards they shook my hand and thanked me for coming.'

'So you got the job?'

He laughed again, and the thunder chose the same time to announce itself. 'They are making me Managing Director on Monday. Don't you see how I am dancing with joy?' He closed his eyes. 'I had so much hope that I would get this job. I answered their questions, did their exam. I have worked for years as a government clerk and can do this job in my sleep. I don't know anyone. All I have is my qualifications and six good years of experience and that's not enough to get a job in government nowadays. I know its bad out there but I never knew this unemployment thing was going to last so long. What am I going to do to provide for you people?' He sighed.

She moved to sit by him and touched his shoulder. 'With God on our side…He will help us. I'm going to prayers tonight and I have been fasting.'

His shoulders shook. 'We have no money for food. That is no longer fasting my friend. That is starvation by force.'

'We must have faith.'

'Faith in what?'

'In God and in knowing that whatever we face, we love each other.'

He put Baby down, looked at her and laughed again. 'I don't believe in God anymore remember.' He pulled her close. 'I still believe in love though. So what do you say? Let's make another baby right here…right now. Let's create our own storm.' His eyes flashed with a wicked fire and her heart started to pound.

'Are you mad?' she asked.

He nodded. 'Isn't that what our parents said when we announced that we wanted to get married?' He pushed her down onto the bed and laughed as she struggled. 'What's wrong? Where is all that love you were talking about before?'

Baby started to cry again as they struggled wordlessly.

'Let me go to my child! Can you not hear him crying?' she pleaded breathlessly as she stopped struggling, realising that it only inflamed matters. Her silence spoke to him as she lay there, hands over her breasts, staring at the ceiling as Baby's distress intensified.

'I am not your enemy you know.'

He sighed and got off the bed, sauntered to the window and watched as the rain beat against the cold concrete floor of the yard. Little puddles widened into pools and pools into little oceans, like the tears of giants. He couldn't afford to let things fall apart. He was a man. He had to be strong for Chinwe. Strong for his son.

'Your mother says that I will never amount to anything as if she thinks I am happy to let my wife wash the neighbours' dirty clothes for money. I have gone for so many interviews and have found nothing. It's like the spirits are working against us, just as your father said they would if we got married.'

Chinwe remembered how her parents had refused to give them their blessing and how they had got married at the Registry with Lanre's widowed mother and one of his uncles as the only witnesses.

'My parents were upset that I hadn't completed my sewing apprenticeship. When I got pregnant, they were disappointed.'

'Do they think that their daughter was the only one who had dreams of how life was supposed to be? They just didn't want you to marry a common *Ngbati* government clerk, so don't tell me about your apprenticeship. Besides, you were quite happy to sneak into my room in those days when we shared the same yard and spend time in my bed when your parents were asleep. I never forced you. It didn't matter to you then that I came from the other side of the Niger River.'

She stood up from the bed and picked Baby up. 'Don't insult me Lanre. My family don't want to know me anymore, yet I am still here with you trying to support you. Yes, even if it means taking in dirty clothes to wash and hearing all the gossips in the street laugh at me.'

He sighed. 'I've heard their laughter too, Chinwe.' His voice gentled a bit then, before silently gazing out of the window again. 'Is there anything to eat?'

She looked at him, seeing him as she had eighteen months ago, as that bright star that had burst into her life, so handsome and clever with his smart pressed khaki trousers and big English. *Broda Akowe* they used to call him in a hushed tone of respect as he was one of the few people in the yard that could read and write English so well. He did have a job then and a big, shiny motorbike that he used to transport people around. He told her he was going to be a Big Man one day and she still believed him.

A Big Man one day. That's what he told her the first day they had met under the mango tree. They had both gone to fetch water at the street tap, got talking, so much talking that she had forgotten the time, while her parents had worried about her whereabouts.

She strode over to him and looked into his eyes. 'I have some *gari* - cassava - I can soak and some groundnuts.'

He shook his head and smiled. '*E go better o.* I will have some small *gari.*' He held out his hands and took back his son. The storm had started to quieten now and Chinwe could hear her own voice singing praise songs to her God as she poured the cassava into a plastic bowl and added water.

'Chinwe.'

'Yes.' She turned around and saw the shadow of a smile on her husband's face as he bent over to play with his son. She served him the food.

'See Chinwe. Our son is now crawling.'

Baby was smiling and clapping his hands at his achievement.

'When?'

'Just now.'

So, they sat and waited and Lanre talked about this job he had seen advertised on the school gates down the road. They urgently needed a janitor and he needed a job.

'Maybe I should see the Headmaster tomorrow. It's not a permanent thing…just to bring something in until I get a real job.'

'Of course.' She nodded and as she did so, she saw Baby turn slowly and move towards her. It was a small move, but it meant so much.

'Did you see that?' Lanre clapped his hands and smiled at his son. 'He is moving forward.'

She felt like clapping too. 'It is a sign from above.'